SOUL SE
PEN AI

Becca Van

MENAGE EVERLASTING

Siren Publishing, Inc.
www.SirenPublishing.com

A SIREN PUBLISHING BOOK
IMPRINT: Ménage Everlasting

SOUL SENTINELS 2: PEN AND PASER
Copyright © 2016 by Becca Van

ISBN: 978-1-68295-286-3

First Printing: June 2016

Cover design by Les Byerley
All art and logo copyright © 2016 by Siren Publishing, Inc.

Printed in the U.S.A.

PUBLISHER
Siren Publishing, Inc.
www.SirenPublishing.com

SOUL SENTINELS 2: PEN AND PASER

BECCA VAN
Copyright © 2016

Chapter One

Paser looked over his shoulder occasionally as he cooked dinner. He and the other sentinels had been watching Set and Sab as they interacted with their mate, Zara for the last six months, and although he liked her just fine, he was envious. He wanted what his friends had, and even though he remembered Ra telling them all they would find their mates, he was impatient to meet the woman meant to be his and Pentu's.

He and Pen had been best friends for thousands of years, and the long, lonely existence got to him sometimes, but since Set and Sab had mated with Zara, he seemed to feel the emptiness in his heart much more than he ever had. By the wistful expression on Pen's face when he saw them talking quietly, he felt the same. There was no need for him and Pen to voice their desires to each other, because after being friends for so long, they could practically read each other's minds.

There were times when Paser wondered if agreeing to be Ra's sentinels had been worth it. Fighting the demonic day after day, week after week, year after year for millennia became a ceaseless fight and at times downright boring. He didn't begrudge keeping humanity safe from the shadow demons, but living and fighting for eternity was starting to weigh on him. Sometimes he wished he could go back to that fated day so long ago when Ra had appeared and offered them immortality and refuse, but he couldn't go back in time, and now that the sun god had said they were going to be rewarded for their loyal service by sending or finding mates for them, he wasn't about to give up.

* * * *

Nina had just finished her shift at the bar she worked at, and although she was tired and her feet were aching, she was full of excitement, but she had no idea why. As she stepped out into the cool night fall air, she inhaled deeply and felt the tension in her shoulders and neck ease.

It was two in the morning and she would have loved to have been able to drive home, but she didn't have the money for a car, so she often rode the secondhand bike she'd picked up at a garage sale a few weeks back or walked. It was only about a mile or so to the apartment complex where she leased a small one-bedroom efficiency, and she liked taking the time it took her to ride or walk home to unwind.

Tonight was different, though, but she couldn't have said why. As she walked along the street, she made sure that there was no one lurking about in the shadows or following her. She'd learned from experience to keep her wits about her. Last month, she'd been mugged by two teenage boys on her way home, and although she'd tried to fight them off, they had been much bigger and stronger than she was. She was lucky enough to have walked away with a few bruises and a grazed cheek when they'd held her face to the ground as they'd stolen all of her tip money.

Those little shits had made it hard for her to get through the week without the extra cash she'd earned, because after paying her rent and bills, she'd barely had enough cash left to buy food. Luckily she was frugal and she'd survived. She'd lived off of peanut butter sandwiches and noodles.

Nina pushed her thoughts aside and thought about the shower she was going to take as soon as she got home, and after she was clean, she was going to go to bed and sleep as long as possible. Tomorrow was Sunday and the only day she allowed herself the luxury of sleeping in. Every other day she got up early to scan the classifieds, looking for extra work so she could get ahead in life.

Nina didn't have any family, so the luxury of her even thinking about attending college after finishing high school had been a pipedream.

The hair on the back of her neck stood on end, making shivers of alarm race up and down her spine. She turned to look behind her and she couldn't see anyone about, but the feeling of being watched remained. Without trying to be too obvious, she dug into her purse and sighed with relief when her hand landed on the can of pepper spray. She withdrew it from her bag, pulled the cap off and clutched the can tightly in her fist.

Nina picked up her pace. She didn't want to break into an all-out run, but with the way she was feeling, maybe she should. Her skin felt like it was crawling with ants and she was panting, but not from exertion. She was scared but had no idea where the threat she felt was coming from. When she turned the corner, the sensation of being watched dissipated, but it came back within seconds. However, when she again looked behind her and all around, she couldn't see anyone.

She thought she saw movement in the park up ahead, but when she squinted and looked harder, nothing moved and she couldn't see anyone lurking in the shadows. Usually Nina walked through the park, but the thought of doing so now gave her the chills, so she changed direction and began to skirt around it.

Tomorrow she would probably laugh at her paranoia and scoff over being scared by the bogey man she hadn't been scared of since she was a little girl, but she was all alone and still couldn't shake the feeling of eyes on her.

As she got to the farther edge of the park, she began to relax. She was no more than two hundred yards from her complex and nothing untoward had happened. Normally she didn't have an overactive imagination, but for some reason, tonight felt different.

Nina froze when she saw something move out from behind the trunk of a large pine tree on the edge of the park, but she couldn't see anything other than what appeared to be a moving shadow. Her heart flipped in her chest and then slammed against her ribs when she realized that the shadow seemed to be moving toward her. She backed up a step and then another, all the time keeping her eyes on that…thing.

When her back connected with a hard body, she whimpered, and as she moved her head to peer at whoever she'd bumped into, she felt as if she were moving in slow motion. Every beat of her heart was loud in her ears and each breath she inhaled wasn't enough to fill her lungs. She had to tilt her head up to look into the guy's face, and when her gaze connected with his, she wished she hadn't. The man's eyes were filled with evil, yet they also appeared to be soulless. That was when she realized that the chest pressed against her back wasn't warm like it should have been. In fact, she couldn't feel any heat coming off of his body at all.

It took every ounce of her determination to lift her foot from the ground and take the first step away from him because she was trembling so hard her knees had actually been knocking together. A bubble of hysterical laughter formed in her chest as she understood an expression she'd once heard from one of the nuns in the convent she'd grown up in. Knee-knocking fear.

She'd always thought that Sister Lysandra had only been trying to scare her and the other girls, but maybe she hadn't been.

Nina froze again when she turned her head face-forward and saw that the shadow she'd seen earlier was hovering so close to her. If she were brave enough to reach out, she would have been able to touch it, but she wasn't that brave, nor that stupid. There was something really weird going on, but she wasn't sure she really wanted to know what. After she managed to bring her other foot next to the first, she tried to shuffle sideways to get out from between the weird man behind her and the floating dark shadow. When she clenched her fists, she felt the can in her right hand and lifted her arm quickly then pressed the button down. A fine mist shot out and straight into the guy's face and eyes. She gulped when he blinked, but the pepper spray didn't seem to have any effect on him whatsoever. He didn't howl in pain or try to rub his eyes.

The sound of eerie laughter hurt her ears, and if she hadn't been so fucking scared, she would have lifted her arms and covered them to keep the screeching sound out. The quaking in her legs moved to the rest of her body when the shadow seemed to form an arm and lift it toward her. Nina couldn't contain her fear anymore. Her heart was pounding so hard she wondered if she would have a heart attack, and that wasn't all. Pain pierced her chest. She felt as if a piece of her was being tugged at, and when she looked down, she saw a small blue light coming from her body.

She screamed as loud as she could, hoping that someone was around and would help her, but she wasn't about to hold her breath. She ducked under the shadow's arm, spun and took off running as fast as she could. The pepper spray can landed with a thud before rolling away.

Another blood-curdling scream left her mouth when a cruel hand gripped her shoulder so hard she knew instant bruises had formed. She twisted and threw one of her own arms up, hoping to knock the hand on her shoulder off, but the man's grip tightened to the point of agony and as his fingers pressed on her collarbone, she wondered if it would snap.

She caught movement in her peripheral vision and felt her mouth drop open when two very tall, very muscular, handsome men appeared out of nowhere, and then they were striding toward her purposefully. Their jaws were set in determination and they looked like what she imagined warriors from the past would look like, except for the modern clothes. They both reached up and over their shoulders and as they pulled their arms back to the front, she saw that they were each holding curved, sickle-like swords in their hands, and the sword blades had a slight golden glow to them.

"Let her go," the one with brown hair demanded as he looked over her shoulder at the evil man gripping her so tightly.

The only way she could describe the shrieking sound that hurt her ears as the man laughed was evilly demonic. When the hand on her shoulder gripped even harder, Nina had to grit her teeth so she wouldn't scream in agony again. She closed her eyes and clenched her jaw so tightly she wondered if she would crack a tooth, but dental work was the least of her worries right now.

A breeze superseded a swishing sound, and when she opened her eyes, it was to see the black-haired man standing in front of her with his sword across his body as if he'd just slashed the air. Her suspicions were confirmed when she saw that the shadow in front of her looked like it had been cleaved in two as it writhed and shrieked as if in pain. How that was possible, she wasn't sure, because the shadow wasn't even substantial enough to be solid, but now wasn't the time for questions. If she got out of this with her life intact then maybe she would start to ask.

The man behind her wrapped his free arm around her neck and began to squeeze. Tears poured down her cheeks and although she clawed at the arm strangling her, it didn't seem to affect the guy trying to kill her.

Nina felt the man hurting her jerk and she somehow knew that she wasn't the one causing him to hurt. His roar of pain hurt her ears, but then, to her relief and surprise, the arm around her neck fell and the grip on her shoulder ceased. If she could have stayed upright, she would have, but she fell to her knees, coughing and gasping as she tried to fill her burning lungs. Her throat was so sore, and even though she felt as if it had been crushed, she could feel her chest expanding and deflating each time she inhaled and exhaled.

When she turned her head, her mouth gaped in horror. The man who'd been holding her had been nearly sliced in two by one of those wickedly sickle-shaped swords, but what scared her beyond reason was that there was no blood and he was still standing.

Nina tried to push to her feet so she could run, but she was trembling so much and feeling weak with fear that she nearly fell flat on her face. She caught herself at the last moment and somehow ended up on her ass. When the evil guy turned and looked at her, her breath stuttered in her throat and she felt frozen with terror. He was smiling at her, but it was the most maliciously evil smile she'd ever seen. The brown-haired man stepped up behind him, and with a fast slice of his sword, he decapitated the evil man.

Nina stared in horror at the macabre scene, and when she heard the screaming, she covered her ears to try and block the horrid sound out. The head rolled toward her and stopped about a yard from where she was sitting on the ground. Acid roiled in her stomach and she turned to the side as she vomited, heaving until there was nothing left to come up.

Darkness closed in around her vision and she pulled in great gulps of air as she tried to remain conscious. Swiping a hand across her mouth, hoping to remove the vile taste didn't help, and she realized her eyes were closed.

The darkness receded and when she heard movement, she opened her eyes and watched with fascinated horror as the body and head turned to ashes. Silence reigned, a slight breeze blew the ash away and for the first time since the horrible screaming had stopped, Nina realized she'd been the one making all the noise.

The two men who'd saved her took a step toward her and before she could stop it, a whimper escaped her mouth. Both men stopped and with slow deliberation, lifted their arms up, the golden, curved blades of their swords gleaming in the soft light of the street lamp she only now became aware of.

She wanted to get to her feet and run as far and as fast as she could, but she was still quaking so much that she felt as weak as newborn foal. She squeezed her eyes closed, waiting for the death blows, but when nothing happened she forced her eyelids up.

The two men stood still and quiet, watching her intently, and it took her a few moments to realize that their hands were now empty. Neither of them held their swords. Her gaze wandered up over their muscular bodies and although she didn't like it, she couldn't seem to help the way her body reacted to their handsome faces and brawny frames.

"We won't hurt you," the brown-haired man said in a low, calm voice, slowly lifting his arms until he held his hands up, palms out in a classic defensive pose.

A bubble of laughter nearly choked her when she swallowed it back down. There was nothing defensive about him or his friend. They could probably snap her neck with a click of their fingers if they so wished to.

"Are you hurt?" the guy with the darker hair asked.

Nina opened her mouth but the word rolling across her mind wouldn't come, so she shook her head. She didn't care that she'd just lied to them. She didn't know them and after what she'd just seen, she wanted to leave, get to her apartment, lock the door and hope that she'd just had a very bad dream. Now that the danger seemed to have passed and the adrenaline was waning in her system, her shoulder was throbbing so much she wasn't so sure that her collarbone wasn't broken. When she felt something warm trickle over her skin, she swiped at it and then looked down at her wet fingers uncomprehendingly.

Blood marred her fingers and the edge of her palm, and although she tried to remember how it got there, her mind was still too frantic to work properly.

She snapped her gaze to the two men when she heard them both take another step toward her and she gasped with pain as she placed her hand back on the ground, trying to scuttle away from them.

"You're hurt." The man with the brown hair stated the obvious, but she remained mute.

"Let us help you," the other said as he crouched down in front of her. "I'm Paser Ebo and he's Pentu Chatha."

What the hell kind of names are those?

"You can call me Pen."

Nina stared at him blankly, but she took in every detail of their features, just in case she got out of this so she could report them to the cops. She wasn't sure these two men were bad, but they certainly weren't angels. They had, however, just saved her life.

Pen's hair looked like it was dark brown, and although she shouldn't have been able to see the color of his eyes in the dim light, she could tell that they were green. He was wearing a faded pair of denim jeans and a black T-shirt, of which the arms were stretched taut over his bulging biceps.

Paser's hair was darker than Pen's, the black tresses a little longer than collar length. When he tilted his head, she was able to see that his eyes were a warm, soulful brown. He was wearing black jeans and a white T-shirt that seemed to set off his dark hair and bronzed skin. The contrast was striking. Both of them were stunningly handsome and no matter how hard she tried to draw her gaze away from their gorgeous manly visages she couldn't seem to.

"What's your name, love?" Paser asked.

Nina opened her mouth to answer, but when only a squeak came out, she had to clear her throat several times before she tried again. "Nina."

"That's a pretty name, Nina…" Pen looked at her expectantly and she swallowed around the constriction in her throat before replying.

"Nina Page."

"Don't be scared of us, Nina. Let us take care of you." Paser held a hand out toward her and she eyed his large hand before lifting her gaze to his again.

When she looked into his eyes, she could see kindness and sincerity. There were creases at the corners of his eyes as if he laughed a lot, and she felt as if she had known him for a long time.

Nina gave a mental snort and wondered if she'd completely lost her mind. Maybe she had and everything she'd seen tonight had been nothing more than the dark recess of her mind conjuring up a gruesome nightmare.

She decided that if this was real and she wasn't having a nightmare then she was well and truly insane, and the only way to find out was to touch. If she could feel then she had to be awake. Right?

Yes, but you can feel when you're dreaming, too, you idiot. That's why dreams and nightmares seem so real and you wake up gasping for breath and your heart racing.

Nina dug her nails into her thigh and bit her lip to keep her gasp of pain contained. She gazed from Paser to Pen and back again. They didn't look frustrated or angry as she stared. Neither of them moved as they waited to see what she would do next.

She knew that if she was awake that she couldn't sit on the cold ground all night and there was no way in hell she wanted to remain outside after what had happened. Come to think of it, she didn't want to be alone at all.

What she needed was a couple of stiff drinks and answers.

However, she wasn't really sure she wanted to hear their replies if she got to ask the questions.

What the hell had the shadow been? What about the man they'd killed? He—it—hadn't even bled when cut by those wicked-looking swords, but it hadn't died straight away, either.

A shiver of fear raced up her spine. Something was really wrong with what had gone down. She'd felt the evil in the air right down to her bones. She hoped to never see anything like what she'd seen again, but she had a bad feeling this was just the beginning.

She wondered how long Paser would hold his hand out toward her before dropping it and walking away. That thought sent disappointment into her gut and she wondered what the hell was wrong with her.

Nina had never reacted to any man the way she was reacting to Pen and Paser, and although that intrigued her, it also worried to hell out of her.

If she didn't know any better, she wondered if she was being set up by one of those shows that punked people to get their kicks. She glanced about her, trying to see if there were cameras hidden anywhere, but drew a deep breath when she knew she was just grasping at straws.

Nina decided that if she had indeed lost her mind then she might as well enjoy the ride. She met Paser's and Pen's gazes and slowly reached out to take Paser's hand. The moment their skin touched, fire sparked into her veins and she drew in a ragged breath. Pen offered her his hand, too, and when their skin connected another spark of desire heated her blood.

They helped her to her feet and she would have fallen if Pen hadn't quickly released her hand and snagged her around the waist.

"I knew you were hurt." Paser frowned at her with concern.

"Will you let us take you back to our home so we can help you?" Pen asked.

Nina shook her head and licked her dry lips. "My apartment complex is just around the next corner."

The moment the words left her lips she cringed. She didn't want these men knowing where she lived. She didn't know them and the adage of them being axe murders flitted across her mind, making her giggle hysterically. They'd already killed one man tonight. They could have their sights set on her to be their next victim.

"Shh, Nina. I promise you're safe with us." Pen brushed the hair back from her face.

"I don't…" Nina squeaked when Paser swept her off her feet, up into his arms and against his warm, hard chest. "What are you doing?"

"I don't want you walking until we're sure you haven't broken anything." Paser met her gaze.

Nina knew she hadn't broken any bones because she didn't like pain, and knew if she had she would be crying like a baby. She inhaled deeply and nearly moaned when she caught a whiff of Paser's sandalwood scent. The cologne or body wash mixed with his natural smell nearly had her eyes rolling back in her head. The combination had the effect on her like she imagined an aphrodisiac would on a nymphomaniac.

Pen moved closer, and when she inhaled through her nose, she whimpered as the desire coursing through her blood ratcheted up another notch. He smelt different to Paser but just as good. He had a more earthy smell to him with a hint of pine fragrance. The combination of the two had her pussy clenching and cream dripping onto her folds. Thank goodness they didn't realize the sound she'd made was because she was turned on. It would have been damn embarrassing if they had.

"We'll have you patched up soon, sweetheart," Pen said as he stroked a finger down her cheek.

"We can't take you back to your place, Nina." Paser glanced about the park and street. "It's not safe."

"What…what's going on?"

"We don't have time to explain right now, love, but I promise we'll explain everything soon." Pen nodded to Paser. "Let's get out of here."

Paser grunted in acknowledgement and then he was moving.

Nina blinked. Everything was a blur and the cool breeze rushing over her skin caused her to shiver. She blinked again and gasped when she opened her eyes. Pen was standing in front of large double metal doors that were the entrance to a small beach house, somewhere she'd never been before. She could smell water and trees, and as she looked about, she had no clue where they were.

The medium-sized beach house gleamed in the rays of the rising sun. She'd never seen such a well-kept house. The paint on the outside was an off-white color and looked fresh with the blue-tinted window surrounds.

What amazed her was that the out-of-place-looking, metal doors which didn't have a lock or a handle. Those doors were an ugly contrast to such a beautiful house and carefully maintained gardens. However, that wasn't what had her staring at the doors. At first she couldn't work out what was missing from them, other than the way they were so different to the rest of the property. And then it hit her. There was no keyhole or handles. She wondered how they were going to open one of the doors but didn't have to wait very long. If she hadn't seen Pen press his finger to a small pad under a bit of plant foliage and then him reaching for the concealed notch to open the doors, she would never have known the lock was there.

There was a lake to her right that sparkled under the illumination of the moon. She sighed at the peacefulness of the scene and the tranquil noise of water lapping against the shoreline. Frogs croaked in amongst the tall, thick reeds near the water's edge and she even heard the quacking of a couple of ducks.

When she looked up, she could see that the sun was just lightening the horizon in the east and wondered where all the time had gone. It had to be close to seven a.m., if not later, and although she knew that time had seemed to freeze when she was confronted by those things, she hadn't been aware that hours had passed by.

Nina didn't really understand why she was being so complacent, but she didn't want to be alone after facing those…things, and there was something about Pen and Paser that drew her to them. It wasn't just because they were handsome and muscular. There was more to it than that, but as she pondered the why of it, the only thing she could come up with was their aura of power and authority. She'd never been attracted to any man like she was to these two, and even though it was way out of the ordinary for her to be so spontaneous, she couldn't seem to help herself.

Pen opened the doors and stepped back to allow Paser to carry her inside. She blinked with fatigue and tried to take everything in, the route he carried her, but she was so exhausted that each time she blinked, her eyes remained closed a little longer.

Even hearing other voices wasn't enough to rouse her from her exhausted stupor, and with a sigh, she gave in and rested her cheek on Paser's shoulder.

Chapter Two

Paser could barely manage to take his eyes off Nina. The moment he'd seen her in the clutches of the demon-possessed body, his heart had raced with fear. Not because an innocent was in danger, although that had been part of it, but because he'd known that she was meant to be theirs.

What worried him the most, however, was the fact that the possessed human hadn't been one of the innocents that Apep's minions usually targeted. He had no idea how the hell the underworld leader had managed to channel his powers to use on those less worthy but it was a big concern. For all they knew, there could be thousands of demons roaming the streets looking for souls to steal, and if that were the case they could be in deep shit. There were only the eight sentinels in total, including him and Set, and they couldn't be everywhere at once.

He wished the other gods had sentinels to help out, but as far as he knew, they didn't. Ra was the only god to have recruited humans to help fight against the underworld and had never mentioned the other gods to him or his friends. He wondered if the other deities even cared about their fight to keep humanity safe.

If Apep's shadows were capable of possessing the less-savory humans, it may not take him long to convene enough to take over the world. They needed to set up a meeting with Ra, the sun god, and warn him about their worries. Hopefully Ra would have a solution or information on what needed to be done to stop Apep from accumulating hordes of evil followers. Maybe they could talk Ra into convincing the other gods to step in and start recruiting their own sentinels. It would certainly make their lives a hell of a lot easier.

"Is she all right?" Pen asked as he opened the door to their apartment.

"I think so. She's fallen asleep." Paser smiled down at the precious bundle in his arms. She looked so small, fragile and angelic with her flushed cheeks, creamy skin and petite yet surprisingly curvy body. His cock stirred, not for the first time tonight, but he pushed his lust aside. Right now, they needed to make sure that Nina wasn't badly hurt.

He strode through their living room and straight for his bedroom, and gently placed her on his bed after Pen had pulled the covers back. "We need to remove her clothes and shoes."

Pen nodded and took one of her small feet into his hand, pulling her black shoe from her foot. Paser did the same with her other foot and then he let his eyes peruse her small frame. Although she wasn't very tall, her legs were long and toned under her blue denim jeans. Her hips were rounded, her belly flat and her waist was small. Her breasts were full and perky, not too big for her petite body, but what drew his gaze more than anything were her rosy, lush lips, long black eyelashes and thick, silky shoulder-length black hair. She looked like a damn pixie compared to him and Pen since they were so much bigger than she was.

With a sigh of resignation, he reached for the buttons on her shirt and started to undo them.

"We should leave her jeans on." Pen helped him release her arms from her shirt before pulling it away.

"Fuck!" Paser snarled when he saw the bruising on her shoulder. It was already a deep black-and-blue color and there were trails of blood on her bra and breast.

"Do you think that asshole cracked her bone?" Pen asked.

"I don't know. Maybe we should have taken her to the hospital."

"Yeah, but she doesn't seem to be in a lot of pain."

"She could be one of those people who have a high tolerance," Paser said. "Let me get some water and disinfectant so we can clean her up. We don't want her getting an infection."

Paser turned toward the bathroom and, after he had what he needed, hurried back to Nina. He cleaned the cuts and blood, and then applied some ointment before covering the gouges with some Band-Aids. Just as he placed the cloth and bowl onto the bedside table, Nina moaned and began to move restlessly. As he reached out to take one of her hands in his, she bolted upright in bed and screamed so loud and long there was no way the other sentinels hadn't heard her. However, he didn't care about that. What he cared about was that Nina was having a nightmare and was scared out of her wits.

Her eyes were wide open but he could tell she wasn't really here and still locked in the terror of her dream. Pen sat on the bed and lifted her into his arms and onto his lap. She fought his friend, her arms flailing and her legs kicking as she tried to fight off her imaginary assailants.

Paser crawled onto the bed, too, caught her wrists and carefully restrained her so she couldn't hurt herself. The door to their apartment burst open and slammed against the wall, and then the others crowded into the room. Pen wrapped his arms around Nina's shoulders, hiding her bra-clad chest from the others' gazes. Paser grabbed the hem of his shirt, tugged it up over his head and then draped it over Nina's shoulders and chest.

Nina tensed and stopped fighting, and Paser could tell by her panting breaths that she had awoken. He was glad she had, but hated that she'd been so scared.

"Is she okay?" Zara asked as she pushed between Set and Sab, moving closer to the bed.

"I think so," Paser managed to answer just before Nina lifted her head from Pen's chest to look toward Zara.

"Hi, I'm Zara." Zara smiled and Paser could tell by the way the smile didn't reach her eyes that she was concerned for Nina.

"Nina," she said in a hoarse voice.

"Why don't you all leave so I can help Nina?" Zara suggested.

Paser didn't want to leave Nina, but when he saw her look down at her bare arms and cotton-covered chest, her cheeks flamed with embarrassment and he decided it may be better to give her some time to compose herself. The reprieve might help him and Pen in their chances of wooing her. So far, she'd been accepting of their help and presence, but he wasn't sure she would remain that way when they told her what they were and what it was they were fighting against to keep humanity safe.

With a sigh of resignation, he glanced at Pen and nodded. With a last, lingering look at her gorgeous yet bemused face, he rose and followed the others out, closing the door behind him. He headed straight for the kitchen, set a pot of coffee brewing and began to prepare for breakfast.

"Is she yours?" Mit asked.

Paser glanced at his friend and nodded. Mit smiled and waggled his eyebrows. "She's a pretty little thing."

"Keep your damn eyes to yourself," Pen snarled as he ran his fingers through his hair.

"What crawled up your ass?" Nehi frowned.

"He's feeling a mite jealous," Paser answered. "I am, too."

"You don't think any of us would try and encroach…" Nehi paused when Pen shook his head.

"Sorry, I don't know why I feel so possessive but I can't seem to help it."

Paser ran his fingers through his hair and sighed. "I think until she's ours, we are going to be a bit unreasonable. I've never felt this way about a woman before."

"Me either," Pen stated. "I hope that she wants to stay."

"I do, too." Paser glanced at Pen.

"What are we going to do if she doesn't?"

"Hell if I know." Paser stopped and stared back toward the door. "One thing I do know for certain is we have to make damn sure we keep her safe."

* * * *

Nina was glad the men had left the room and quickly slipped the large T-shirt on. It was so big it kept slipping off her shoulder, but that was the least of her worries. She couldn't believe she'd let Paser and Pen bring her back to their place without putting up a fuss. Normally she was very wary of strangers, but for some reason she couldn't help but trust the two men. Maybe it was because they had saved her life tonight.

However, now that she wasn't scared out of her mind, she had so many questions but no one to ask. Or maybe she did.

Zara sat on the end of the bed and met her gaze. "Have they told you anything yet?"

"What about?"

"I'll get back to that in a minute. What happened to you?"

Nina shuddered and wrapped her arms around her waist. She explained what she remembered to Zara.

"Shit! That's not good."

Nina frowned, and although she agreed with Zara, she had feeling that Zara's statement was for a totally different reason than what she was thinking.

"None of this makes sense." Nina got off the bed and began pacing. "If I didn't know any better, I'd think that the shadow I saw was an evil spirit or something."

"'Or something' is right."

"How did Paser and Pen kill a shadow, and why didn't the man who tried to hurt me die right away?"

Nina took a deep breath and tried to calm down, but it didn't work. She was scared out of her mind and her imagination was working overtime. Add in the fact that Pen and Paser moved faster than was humanly possible, and it made her think that they had superpowers or something, but that sort of thing only happened in the movies. Didn't it?

"What the hell is going on?"

Zara stood and clasped Nina's hand before leading her back to the bed. Both of them sat down and Zara took a deep breath as if shoring up her resolve.

"Have you ever heard of Ra?"

"Yeah. Who hasn't? He was an ancient Egyptian."

"Yes. He is the sun god."

A shiver of apprehension traversed Nina's spine and she looked at Zara incredulously.

"I know what you're thinking, but I'm not crazy and neither are you. That shadow was from the underworld and quite probably one of Apep's demonic minions."

"You can't be serious." Nina started laughing because if she didn't laugh, she would likely start screaming.

"Let me finish, Nina." Zara broke into her hysteria.

Nina took few deep breaths and sighed when she felt some of the tension in her muscles dissipate. "Go on." She would listen to Zara, but after that, she was out of here.

"Back in the time when the pyramids were being built, the pharaohs enslaved men to use them to build their temples and tombs. The slaves were abused until they could no longer work, and if that happened, they were usually whipped to death. When an elderly man fell to his knees, eight men stepped in to protect him and, by doing so, angered the pharaoh. The pharaoh ordered that the eight men would take the elderly man's punishment, thus saving his life.

"Ra, the sun god, had been watching the greedy pharaohs, and as soon as he saw the injustice about to happen, he stepped in. The pharaoh's overseers and the pharaoh himself were whipped to death."

"What happened to the men?"

"The eight men were recruited by Ra to fight Apep's shadow demons. They were turned into demigods and continue to fight to this day."

Nina stared at Zara. Surely she didn't mean Paser, Pentu and the six others were those men. That would mean they had been alive for thousands of years. That just wasn't possible.

She chuckled and then started laugh so hard she could barely draw a breath. Tears leaked from her eyes and down her cheeks. When she glanced at Zara and saw the woman was watching her with a concerned but very serious expression, she realized that Zara believed everything she'd just said. Nina's hysterical laughter stopped abruptly. She rose and hurried toward the door.

"I'm not lying or making this up, and I'm not crazy," Zara said in a calm voice.

"You expect me to believe this shit."

"Yes."

"I think you should go see a doctor."

"If I'm lying, how did Pen and Paser kill a shadow and the other guy?"

"It was probably all a set-up."

"Why?" Zara flung her hand out in exasperation. "Do you know them? Have you ever seen them before tonight?"

"No."

"Then why would you think someone you don't know would go to such elaborate lengths for a prank? And if you hadn't ever met them before, how would they have known you would be where you were when you were?"

Nina's knees buckled and she leaned against the wall beside the door so she didn't fall to the floor. "What else am I supposed to think?"

"I understand why you're having a hard time believing any of this. I was where you are not so long ago, but I assure you that I'm telling you the truth."

"So Pen and Paser and the others are demigods fighting against Apep's demons?"

"Yes."

"There's only one problem with that."

"What?" Zara tilted her head.

"I didn't see any demons. I saw a shadow and an evil man."

"Did the shadow get close to you?"

Nina nodded and shivered as she remembered feeling really cold, but that wasn't all. She hoped to never encounter another floating shadow in her life. She wasn't sure she could handle being close to that—whatever that had been—again.

"Did you feel a painful tugging sensation in your chest?"

Nina began to tremble again. She hadn't told Zara about that when she'd explained what had happened. She didn't answer but stared at the other woman in shock.

"I can see by your expression that you did. It's terrifying, isn't it? Feels as if a piece of your soul is being ripped out of your body."

Nina sank down the floor. She was shaking so hard now that there was no way in hell she could have remained on her feet. She felt as if she was in a living nightmare and prayed that she would wake up soon.

"Apep uses his demonic shadows to prey on the innocent. The demons need to feed on the souls of humans so they can take and possess humans. The evil god's aim is to take over the world and kill off humanity."

"Why?" Nina asked, her voice barely a whisper.

"Power. Greed. Who knows how evil beings think or work?" Zara shrugged.

"How do you know all of this?"

"My soul was nearly stolen by the demonic." Zara shuddered and wrapped her arms around her waist. "Every night I had the same nightmare of having my spirit ripped out, but I would wake up just in time. If it hadn't been for my mates Set and Sab, I would have been possessed and died."

"Oh God."

"You're in danger, Nina. You can't go home. The only place you'll be safe is here."

"And where is here?"

"You don't know? I thought you were awake when they brought you in."

"I was, but I was in shock. I had just watched Pen and Paser kill a man and a shadow."

"A man?"

Nina nodded. "I can't…I think…" She took a deep breath and released it slowly. Nina felt as if she was going insane, and yet she knew she was as sane as she'd ever been.

"Shit!"

"What?"

"I've learned the shadows only use innocent men and women to steal souls from, but there's a possibility that Apep has figured out how to use evil men to do his bidding."

"The man who hurt me definitely wasn't innocent. In fact, his gaze looked evil to the core." Nina drew her knees up close to her body and wrapped her arms around them. "I don't think he was alive."

"Why do you say that?"

"When Pen and Paser slashed him with their swords, there was no blood, and the first strike should have sent him to the ground but it didn't."

Zara frowned with concern.

"There's more."

"Go on."

"When Pen and Paser killed him, all that was left was ash."

Zara nodded. "Do you believe me now?"

"I'm starting to."

"I promise you I'm not lying. I know it's hard to take in, but it's all true."

"So what am I supposed to do? I can't put my life on hold. I need to work to pay rent and bills."

"You don't need to worry about that. I'm sure your mates will take care of everything."

"Excuse me?" Nina knew her mouth was gaping open. She was so flabbergasted at what Zara had just said. Surely she couldn't have heard right.

"Oh." Zara covered her mouth and blushed.

Nina finally managed to close her mouth and swallowed around the lump in her throat. She met Zara's gaze and shook her head.

"I'm sorry," Zara said. She rose and then came and sat next to Nina. "You had no idea, did you?"

"No! What makes you think I'm their mate? And what the hell do you mean by 'mate,' anyway?"

"Exactly what I said."

Nina shook her head and Zara nodded.

"That's not possible. I don't even know them."

"Are you attracted to them?"

Nina lowered her head, pressing her forehead against her knees.

"I can tell by your silence that you are. Are you a virgin, Nina?"

"What has that got to do with anything?"

"Everything."

"What? Are you trying to tell me that because I haven't had sex that is the reason those two men think I'm their mate?" Nina asked incredulously.

"Don't be ridiculous," Zara snapped with what sounded like frustration.

"Then please enlighten me."

"I will, if you'll give me the chance." When Zara sighed, Nina could tell it was from exasperation.

"Well?"

"I already told you the demonic prey on the innocent."

Nina had forgotten about that. She shivered with remembered fear, but she wasn't sure she wanted to hang around here. She would lose her job and apartment, and then she would have nowhere to live. That was if she came out of any of this intact or alive.

That was the moment of realization for Nina. She knew then with certainty that every word Zara had told her rang true. That didn't mean that the story was believable, just that Zara believed what she'd said.

"How the hell do you know I'm their mate?" Nina cringed at the way she'd blurted out that question. It had been spinning around in her mind and she hadn't known she was going to voice it until she heard herself speaking the words.

"They are very attracted to you."

"Okay," Nina said skeptically.

"I could tell by the way they looked at you."

"How's that?"

"Possessively."

"You can't know that for sure."

"Yeah, I can. I do. It's the same way my mates Set and Sab look at me."

"Maybe you need glasses."

"I see perfectly fine, thank you." Zara smiled and then she chuckled. "You can deny it all you like, but you look at them the same way they look at you."

Nina threw her hands up in the air. "So what? I've probably looked at hundreds on handsome men the same way."

"Did they heat your blood and make your body tingle the way Pen and Paser do?"

Nina looked away when she felt her cheeks heat and hoped her face wasn't too red, but suspected that it was when she saw Zara grin at her from the corner of her eye.

"Wait a minute." Nina met Zara's gaze again. "How the hell could I be their mate? If what you said is true then they're demigods and must be immortal if they've been alive for so long. Even if I am their...mate"—she paused to lick her dry lips—"there is no way in hell a relationship would work. They wouldn't even want to look at me, let alone touch me. I'll be old and wrinkled and they won't have aged at all. That is, if I even believed any of this."

"If you agree to be with them, they can change you." Zara nudged Nina's shoulder.

"What? How? Wait!" Nina scrambled to her knees, crawled across the floor and pulled herself up onto the bed. Her ass was getting sore from sitting on the hard floor. "I don't think you should answer that. I'm not sure I want to know."

"Are you sure?" Zara asked, and although she tried to hide the smile forming on her lips, she wasn't successful.

Nina sighed. "No."

A full-fledged grin formed on Zara's lips and she nodded her head. "If you do decide to become their mates, they will make love to you and bite you with their fangs."

"Fangs?" Nina whispered and felt all the blood drain from her face. Her heart stuttered and then beat a rapid staccato inside of her chest, and she began to pant.

"They have fangs? What are they? Vampires?" Each word she spoke became more strident than the last until she felt as if she were practically screeching. She became lightheaded to the point where she thought she was about to pass out and quickly held her breath. She counted to five and then slowly released the air from her lungs before drawing in another breath. She hadn't realized that she'd closed her eyes until she heard Zara move.

"No, they aren't vampires. What made you come to that conclusion?"

"Oh, gee I don't know. Maybe the fact you said they would bite me with their fangs." The last word was said in a near shout and Nina inhaled raggedly, trying to quell the panic taking hold.

"Shit! Sorry. Don't panic. They aren't vampires and they don't drink blood. Well, not often, anyway."

Nina couldn't handle another word. She stood and hurried toward the door. She must have blinked, or maybe because she was feeling weak with fear, she hadn't moved as fast as she thought, because just as she was reaching for the door handle, she noticed that Zara was leaning against it. The woman had been across the other side of the room and she couldn't possibly have gotten there before Nina. Her mouth gaped open and she began backing away from her. She didn't stop until the back of her knees bumped into the edge of the mattress. When her legs gave out, she didn't do anything to stop her fall. She bounced a couple of times, and although she tried to speak, nothing came out of her mouth.

"Don't look at me like that," Zara said gently. "I won't hurt you."

"I never thought you would."

"Yeah, right. That's why you backed away from me and look like I was about to murder you."

"I never thought any such thing."

"Can I sit?" Zara indicted the spot next to Nina on the bed and she nodded.

"Okay, let me try and explain a little better. I'm sorry if I scared you. That wasn't my intention."

"You didn't scare me, exactly, just shocked me. How did you get to the door before I did?"

"I'll get to that." Zara inhaled deeply and released the breath before she started explaining. "As I was about to tell you, the guys aren't vampires and don't live off of blood. They eat and drink just like anybody else. They will occasionally take a little blood if they are injured in battle. Doing so helps heal their wounds faster. They don't kill anybody they drink from if they're innocent and usually only take blood from their enemies. If you did agree to be their mate, they would bite you while making love to you. I don't know how it works, but if they do that, it connects you to them and you will go through a transformation of sorts."

"What sort of transformation?" Nina asked in a hoarse voice.

"You would end up like them."

"Like them?"

"You wouldn't age as a normal human does. Something in their bite changes our DNA somehow. I'm not a scientist so I don't know the specifics. However, you will live for a very long time. You will be stronger, faster and your senses will be more enhanced. You will also get fangs, but don't worry. They only emerge in times of extreme emotion."

"Such as?"

Zara's face turned pink and she looked away before meeting Nina's gaze again. "Passion, mainly."

"I don't know about this." Nina buried her face in her hands.

Zara patted her shoulder. "You don't have to decide anything right now, but one thing is certain. You can't go home. Not if you want to stay alive."

Nina didn't say anything when Zara got up and walked toward the door. She paused in doorway and met her gaze again.

"I know this is very hard to digest and in such a short span of time, but just remember that those two men will do everything in their power to protect you. They have been alone for thousands of years fighting against a never-ending cause, and all because they stepped in to save a fellow slave. They have more compassion in their little fingers than most men have in the whole bodies. They will also go out of their way to make sure you are happy and loved."

Nina didn't reply, and when Zara closed the door behind her, she curled up on the bed and hugged the pillow to her chest. She was absolutely exhausted and not just because the night was over. Her mind was in turmoil and she had no idea what to think or where to turn.

She hoped that after a few hours of sleep, she would be able to think clearly.

Chapter Three

Pen and Paser hadn't bothered to go to bed. They were both too twisted up inside to even contemplate sleeping. When Zara had come out to the kitchen and nodded her head at them, they knew she had told Nina what they were. He hadn't heard any screaming—although he had heard Nina's raised voice, even if he hadn't actually heard what she'd been saying—so he figured she'd taken the news a hell of a lot better than he would have if he'd been in her position. The other sentinels had retired to their apartments hours ago, and although he had wanted to adjourn to theirs, he and Paser had remained in the kitchen chatting over inconsequential things and drinking coffee, both deliberately ignoring the topic uppermost in their minds.

Pen knew the moment Nina entered the room. Goose bumps raced over his skin and the hair at his nape stood on end. It was the hardest thing he'd ever done to remain sitting in his seat at the table. His first instinct was to leap up from his chair, race over to her and pull her into his arms, but he didn't want to frighten her away. He had a feeling that Nina wouldn't appreciate his display of affection since they'd barely spoken to each other since they'd met.

Paser took a deep breath and stood. Pen held his breath and hoped his friend didn't do anything stupid. He didn't realize he was holding his own breath until Paser walked toward the kitchen part of the room and he released the air in his lungs.

When he looked toward the door, he saw the frown on Nina's face and wanted more than anything to know what she was thinking, but that wasn't about to happen. Her body language was showing all the "keep off" signs with her arms crossed beneath her breasts. She looked so small, lost and vulnerable. His heart ached for her and again he had to push the urge to go to her away.

He decided that maybe talking to her would ease her tension. "How did you sleep, Nina?" If he hadn't been watching her so closely, he would have missed the shiver that made her small body tremble slightly, and he hoped more than anything it was a reaction to his voice, and his and Paser's presence.

"Okay." She sighed, and when she looked away, he knew she lied, but until she got to know them, he wasn't about to call her on the fabrication. Plus, he could see the dark smudges beneath her eyes, a testament to her fib.

"Are you hungry, little one?" Paser asked as he rummaged in the fridge for the breakfast ingredients.

"Yes."

"Take a seat. I'll have breakfast ready soon." Paser dumped the ingredients on the counter and turned to smile at Nina.

The corners of her mouth tilted up but then the frown returned. "I can help. I'm not used to being waited on."

"It would be my honor to cook for you, and besides, I usually do the cooking for everyone." Paser dropped the bacon into a large pan and then started on the eggs.

"Come and sit." Pen patted the seat next to him, and to his surprised pleasure, she came and sat right next to him. "Did Zara tell you about…"

"Yes," Nina answered quickly and then lowered her head.

"Do you believe her, Nina?" Pen asked.

"I don't know," she whispered. "It's all so…fantastical. Like something out of a sci-fi movie."

"If you have any questions, we will answer them to the best of our ability," Paser said.

"I don't even know where to begin."

"Just say whatever is on your mind, Nina. We won't get offended." Pen could feel the heat of her body radiating out toward him. He could also smell her wonderful vanilla scent and her arousal. His cock jerked against the zipper of his jeans and he shifted in his seat, but the move didn't help to relieve the constriction on his hard dick. He knew that Nina was the only one who would be able to relieve him, but she had to accept them as her mates before he touched her. He wasn't sure he could stop if he started.

"How can I be your...mate? I don't even know you."

"About six months ago, Ra told us that he would reward us for our service and loyalty. He told us would find the other half to our souls."

Nina lifted her head and met his gaze. "So you're telling me that without Ra's interference we probably wouldn't be attracted to each other?"

"No. I don't think that's the case," Pen answered, trying to keep the frustration from his voice.

"Then what? It sounds to me like your sun god had a hand in this attraction, and if that is the case, we may not have even been attracted to each other without his influence."

"There is no way Ra could change someone's feelings, Nina," Paser said as he brought over a cup of coffee, placed it in front of her and then put milk and sugar close enough for her to reach if she needed it.

"How do you know that? He's a god, isn't he? He could probably do anything he wants to."

"If we had met under other circumstances, would you have found us attractive?" Pen nudged her chin up with his finger when she looked down at the table. When her face tinged pink with embarrassment he had his answer, but still needed to hear her say the words.

"Yes. How can you ask that? You're both tall, handsome and sexy. You have muscular physiques and could probably grace the cover of any magazine."

"Are you normally attracted to good-looking men the way you are to us?" Paser pushed the jug of milk toward her when she reached for it.

Nina added a little milk to her coffee, stirred and then wrapped her hands around the mug. Paser raced across the room and began to remove the bacon from the pan. Nina's mouth dropped open as she stared at Paser. Her eyes wondered over Pen's friend from head to toe and paused when she got to his ass. Pen bit the inside of his cheek to stop the smile tugging at his lips. She must have seen him watching her from the corner of her eyes because she glanced toward him and then looked down at her coffee again. This time, her face went bright red instead of a slight pink hue.

"Are you going to answer the question?" Pen prodded.

Nina shook her head and then, to his relief, she met his gaze and answered verbally. "No, I'm not normally this attracted to strange, good-looking men."

"We don't react to other women this way either, baby," Pen said.

"I just don't know what to think about...all this. It's just too…surreal."

Pen heard the other sentinels and Zara heading toward them and knew he didn't have long to reply, but he needed Nina to relax and feel comfortable in his and Paser's presence. He covered one of her hands with his and quelled the jolt of attraction from showing.

"We would never hurt you, Nina, nor would we do anything you didn't want. We don't expect you to agree to be ours right away. We'll give you all the time you need."

Nina released a long sigh and nodded. Pen removed his hand from hers just as the others began to file in. Sometimes he hated that they all had enhanced hearing and could discern conversations from far away, but this time he was grateful the others had given them some alone time with their mate. He'd heard Set, Sab and Zara coming toward them earlier, but they had turned back around and given him, Paser and Nina privacy.

He nodded to Set and Sab when their gazes met, and would have acknowledged Zara, too, but she was looking at Nina. "Are you okay, Nina?"

"Yeah, thanks," Nina replied.

Everyone sat down and Pen introduced Nina to the other sentinels. After Paser brought the food over, they began to eat. When Pen saw Nina wince as she moved, he knew she was in pain. "How's your shoulder?"

"Sore, but better than it was."

"Maybe we should take you to see a doctor?" Paser suggested.

Nina shook her head. "No, I'm fine, just bruised."

"You could have a fracture," Zara said.

"No, I don't. I've fractured my collarbone before, so I know I would be in a lot worse pain if that were the case. I'm fine, don't worry."

"Have you ever encountered the demonic before last night, Nina?" Set asked.

"No, and I hope I never do again. I've never been so scared in my life." Nina shivered with remembered fear.

Pen hated her seeing her scared and needed to comfort her. He placed his arm around her shoulders and hugged her. She looked up and met his gaze, and when he saw the desire in her eyes, he nearly lowered his head and kissed her. If Paser hadn't cleared his throat, he probably would have done so in front of everyone else and forgotten they were even there.

Nina's cheeks grew pink and when she shrugged her shoulders, dislodging his arm from around her, he clenched his jaw. He felt rejected and pain pierced his heart. The others talked about what they were going to do for the day, and although he listened, he didn't join in.

"I need to go home," Nina blurted out.

The pain Pen felt a moment ago was pale in comparison to the piercing agony stabbing into his chest, and from the ragged breath he heard Paser draw in, his friend was in much the same condition. He didn't want to let Nina out of his sight, and not just because he wanted her so badly his entire body was aching, but because of his natural inclination to keep an innocent safe.

"Why?" Sab asked before Pen could refute her proclamation.

"I don't have any clothes."

"Are you going to come back here?" Zara asked.

"Yes. There is no way in hell I'm staying at my place alone if I've been targeted by those…things."

Relief and elation surged through Pen. She wasn't trying to get away from him and Paser. He gave a slight nod to Zara, thanking her for getting the information he most wanted from his mate.

"We can take you home to get some stuff, but it's really not necessary." Paser pushed his empty plate aside and leaned back in his chair. "We can buy you whatever you need."

"Thanks for the offer, but no."

"Why not?" Pen asked. "We can afford to get you anything you want. We've accumulated a mass of money over our lifetime and getting you a new wardrobe wouldn't even put a dent in it."

"That's not the point," Nina snapped, inhaling deeply before releasing the breath slowly. "I pay my own way."

"Of course you do," Pen said quickly, trying to appease her ruffled feathers, "but we would love to help you out. We aren't going to hold spending our money on you over your head, baby."

"We like you, Nina and we want to help you."

Nina nodded. "Thank you. I'm sorry I jumped to the wrong conclusions."

"Where do you work, Nina?" Zara redirected the conversation.

"The Province Pub in Price. Shit! I'm going to need to call my boss. He's going to be so pissed off at me. Maybe I can still go to work."

"No, not happening, sweetheart," Paser said. "If you're working and we need to go fight some of the demonic, you would be a sitting duck."

"But surely I'd be safe surrounded by people."

"No, you wouldn't." Pen ran his fingers through his hair. "If Apep has worked out how to use unsavory characters so his shadow demons can possess their bodies that means that the demonic could be more in number than we first suspected. The prick was only ever able to use the innocent until recently. Any disreputable person could be a threat to you."

"Why?" Nina asked.

"Why what?"

"Why are they doing this?"

"Evil is always looking for ways to rule and conquer. Ultimate power is the goal. If Apep succeeds, humanity as we know it will cease to exist and he would end up destroying the world."

"He wants to be able to bring the underworld to the surface?"

"Yes, and if that happens, we're all doomed," Set said.

"What am I going to do about my apartment? I won't be able to pay the rent or bills if I can't work."

"You can move in here," Paser stated. "We can store whatever you want in the warehouse section of our home and you can stay in our spare room."

"For how long?" Nina asked.

"For as long as you like, baby," Pen answered and hoped like hell she would end up staying for eternity.

"Thank you. I'll try to find a way to repay you when this is all over." Nina rose and began to collect the dirty dishes.

"Leave them, sweetheart." Paser took the plates from her hand.

"You cooked. The least I can do is clean up."

"We'll do it," Mit and Wen said at the same time.

"It was our turn anyway." Wen smiled at her.

"Thank you."

"Are you ready to go, Nina?" Pen asked as he stood.

"I would really love to get changed into clean clothes, but since that isn't an option, I'll just go and brush my teeth."

"We'll wait for you here."

Nina nodded before hurrying away. Pen slumped back into his chair and ran a hand over his face.

"She'll come around, Pen," Zara said.

"I hope you're right."

"She's attracted to us." Paser walked toward the door.

"Yeah, but is the attraction enough to sway her decision?" Pen asked.

Chapter Four

The more Nina was near Pen and Paser, the more attracted she became. After they had brought her to her apartment, there was no way she could refute what she'd been told about them and the other sentinels. Once they'd stepped outside, Pen had lifted her up into his arms and taken off. The speed they'd traveled at had been phenomenal and she'd had to close her eyes or she'd have ended up getting sick as the world blurred by.

It had taken them so little time to get to her place and now she was packing a bag with the clothes she would need. When they had followed her in after she'd unlocked the door, she had looked at her home with new eyes and cringed at the coldness of it.

Nina had never had much money and thankfully had leased the one-bedroom apartment fully furnished, but as she'd looked about she thought it looked bleak and tired. Her home wasn't really a home at all. It was just some place to lay her head whenever she got tired or prepare a meal when she was hungry. There were no soft cushions, knickknacks or photos to break up the dull beige décor. There was an old orange sofa which sagged because the springs were gone and the stuffing in the cushions was almost nonexistent.

She hadn't even been able to afford to buy a new mattress but had instead bought a plastic sheet and mattress protector to cover it in case there were any nasties lurking in the material. All she had were the clothes in the closet, which didn't even half-fill the single cupboard, and the few bits and pieces in the dresser.

Until this moment, she'd never realized how she hadn't really been living. She'd been existing from one paycheck to the next barely making ends meet. Thankfully, Pen and Paser didn't say anything as she quickly stuffed her things into her bag. Now that she was done, all that was left was to inform the landlord she was leaving and call her boss to tell him she was quitting.

"Do you have everything?" Pen brushed her hand aside when she would have lifted the battered case from the bed.

"Yes."

"I just need to go and tell the landlord I won't be coming back and hand over the keys."

"I'll come with you," Paser said.

"No, that's okay. I can do it myself." Nina didn't want either of them speaking to her landlord. The guy was a dick and would no doubt give her hell for breaking her lease. There was no way in hell he was going to give her the bond back. "I won't be long."

Nina headed out and when she got to the landlord's door, she took a deep, fortifying breath before knocking.

The door was practically pulled off its hinges when it was opened, and it took everything she had not to grimace. Ted Frost was one of the most disgusting people she'd ever had the misfortune to meet. His beer gut was so big that his dirty, stained T-shirt didn't even cover it, and he wore loose track pants low on his hips, but it was the body odor wafting from him that nearly made her gag. "What?"

Luckily she'd pulled the apartment key from her keyring so she wouldn't have to hang around too long to get it off. She held the key up and toward him as she spoke. "I'm leaving."

"What? You can't. Your lease isn't up."

"I know but I don't expect the bond back."

"Too right, you little bitch. I could sue you for everything you've got."

"Go right ahead," Nina dropped the key at his feet. "I don't have anything so you'd lose in long run."

Nina turned away when his face began to get red and the vein in his head throbbed with his rising ire. She didn't even make it one step away before he grabbed her arm in a cruel grip. She turned back ready to knee him in the balls to get away, but he was a lot stronger than his fat body looked, and before she knew it, she was being dragged into his messy, dirty apartment.

"Let me go," Nina yelled and tugged at her arm, trying to get away.

"You owe me, you little slut. You can pay me on your back."

Fear skittered up Nina's spine and she was about to let loose with a scream loud enough to wake the dead. She'd already drawn in a lungful of air, but as she opened her mouth to scream, she was set free.

Pen had her landlord by the scruff of his shirt and, without any effort, lifted the prick from his feet. Paser wrapped his arms around her waist and pulled her back against him.

"Are you all right? Did he hurt you?" Paser asked.

"No, I'm fine."

Pen turned to look at her. His eyes ran over her body and stopped when he got to her arm. She looked down to see that she had red marks where her landlord had gripped her hard.

"You think you're tough picking on someone smaller than you?" Pen snarled his question. "Only cowards hurt women. If I ever hear you've hurt someone smaller or weaker than you again, you'll regret it."

Nina couldn't see Pen's face after he turned away from her, but whatever he did scared the shit out of her landlord. The strong scent of urine permeated the air and she had to cover her mouth and nose so she wouldn't gag. Pen turned to face her and that was when she saw the fangs, but instead of scaring her, the sight of his elongated teeth and murderous expression ramped up her libido.

She didn't even know she'd moved until she felt her ass pressing back against Paser's thighs and he moaned. That was when she felt the hard ridge of his cock against her lower back, and this time, when she began to pant, it wasn't from fear.

Pen dropped Ted, and when he landed on his knees in his own filth and whimpered, Nina nearly laughed. He was just a yellow-bellied coward, after all. The last twelve months had been hard on her because he was the worst kind of bully. It had been lucky for her to have been working nights at the pub, which made it easier for her to avoid him, since the asshole worked during the day.

He had been gone most of the time before she'd even got out of bed, and she'd always made sure to skirt around the apartment complex in case he'd been watching for her as she'd left for work, if he'd been home. Some of the other women hadn't been so lucky and had had to fight of the slob's advances. Nina had been worried the bastard would end up raping one of them, but she didn't think that was going to be a problem anymore.

Paser shifted his hold on her, lifted her into his arms, cradling her against his chest, and carried her out. Pen followed, slamming the door behind him.

"Show me your arm, baby," Pen demanded.

Nina lifted her arm and gasped when he gently clasped her appendage, running his thumb over the red welts, but not because he'd hurt her. The more they touched her, the more her body responded and she wasn't sure she could hold out for much longer. Her pussy was hot, wet and achy, and her nipples were throbbing. If she'd been standing, her knees would have buckled beneath her when he lifted her arm to his mouth and kissed the red skin, but when he licked the marks with his tongue, she whimpered with a need so intense she felt like she was about to come.

"Let's get out of here," Paser said in a deep, raspy voice that sent another bout of shivers up her spine.

Pen released her arm and looked at her with such a hungry, heated gaze her skin should have been singed from her body. It was only when he bent down and picked up her bag she hadn't noticed outside the door that she as able to draw a deep breath. However, that breath wasn't enough to slow her racing heartbeat or the shallow panting.

"Close your eyes, sweetheart."

That was the only warning she got before they were on the move. The wind felt wonderful on her heated face and hot body, and she hoped by the time they got back to the sentinels' home she would have her desire for them under control again, but she had a feeling that wasn't going to be the case.

Nina opened her eyes when Paser stopped and she clutched at him as he lowered her feet to the ground. She had to order herself to let him go and take a step back because all she wanted to do was cling. She'd never been a clinging vine before, and although she thought that she was becoming attached to him and Pen and should be worried about it, she wasn't. The urge to touch them, kiss them and find out what they tasted like was nearly more than she could stand.

They were both staring at her and she wondered what they saw. What made her so different from any other woman? Why did they think she was their mate? She wondered if they liked the way she looked. When she looked in the mirror, she didn't see anything exceptional or anything to make her stand out from the crowd. She knew she wasn't ugly, but she didn't think she was beautiful. Maybe passably pretty, but that was all.

The silence became fraught with tension and she shifted from foot to foot, uncomfortable. She'd lowered her head again, not because she felt she was lesser than they were, but because she couldn't continue looking into their heated gazes. Her breathing was shallow and rapid, and if they had better hearing than the average person, maybe they could hear her fast heartbeat, too. She hoped that wasn't the case, because if they did, they would know that they affected her equilibrium. Then she remembered Zara saying that once she was mated to them—if she decided she would agree to be theirs—all of her senses would be more exceptional than they already were. If that was so, did that mean they could smell her arousal?

Her cheeks flamed with heat and she knew she was probably red, but there was nothing she could do about that right now.

She startled when a callused finger nudged her chin up, and when she looked into Paser's eyes, she could see that they had a slight yellow glow behind his normal irises. Was that because he—*they* were demigods? She nearly groaned with frustration but not because she needed their touch, although that was also true, but because she still didn't know that much about them.

That was something else that worried her. Would they still want to be with her once they got to know her? She wasn't a horrible person, but she had no experience dealing with men or with relationships. What would happen to her if they decided, after they were mated, that they didn't like her personality at all? Would she be pushed out to fend for herself once more? End up alone like she had been for her whole life?

"What's wrong, sweetheart?"

"That's what I was wondering."

"We need to process your thumbprint so you can open the door if you ever need to." Pen came up behind her and wrapped an arm around her waist.

She shivered at the heat coming off of his body and inhaled deeply of his spicy, manly scent. They both smelled so good she wanted to breathe them in until she had their flavors coating her taste buds and etched into body, mind and soul indelibly.

Paser moved a step forward and cupped her face in his hands. As he stared down into her eyes, all thought fled until all that was left inside her was need, a need so great she wasn't sure she could endure it any longer. His brown eyes got that ethereal inner glow, and just as she opened her mouth to ask why their eyes seemed to take on an inner light, he breached the gap and lowered his mouth to hers.

Nina moaned at the first brush of his lips on hers and, without conscious thought, tangled her fingers into the soft cotton of his shirt. When he nipped her bottom lip, she gasped and then his tongue was inside of her mouth. She felt as if she were drowning, drowning in a sea of heat, taste and desire.

Paser's tongue rubbed along and then twirled around hers. Her legs began to tremble and her knees buckled under her first taste of real passion. Low down in her belly, liquid heat pooled and her pussy became very wet. Her internal muscles clenched, sending a gush of cream to coat her folds, and her nipples ached and hardened.

She mewled when he angled her head for a better fit and he deepened the kiss. She was hungry for more but wasn't sure if leaping into a relationship with two men she barely knew was the right thing to do.

Whether she stiffened at the thought, she wasn't sure, but as Paser slowed the kiss and then lifted his mouth from hers, it took every bit of her will to keep from begging him to kiss her again.

Pen's hands moved to her hips and turned her around to face him. She barely got her eyes open after the passionate kiss she'd shared with Paser before he slanted his mouth over hers. She groaned as the flavor of man and desire exploded on her taste buds, and if he hadn't been holding her up she was sure she would have fallen to the ground at his feet.

Pen's kiss was rapacious and greedy, demanding responses from her she never knew she had, but he also gave. His tongue stroked along and dueled with hers and she couldn't help but to respond in kind.

A whimper escaped her mouth when he broke the kiss, and although she opened her eyes, her vision was blurry from a passionate haze. Pen released her after a couple of heartbeats and as he moved to the side she realized she wasn't the only one breathing heavily. Feminine pride surged through her that her response had caused that reaction, but she quickly quelled it and lowered her gaze to the ground. She didn't want them seeing how much they affected her but suspected they already knew. Confusion warred in her heart and brain. Nina had never had a relationship and didn't really know how to respond to what had just happened. Nor did she want to come across as a femme fatale. More confident than she really was because that was so far from the truth.

She almost jumped when Paser clasped her hand and lifted it, but she was able to suppress the telling action. She didn't want to give them any more of a reason to become complacent or overeager about her or her decisions, because she wasn't sure what she was going to do herself.

Paser pressed her thumb to a pad next to the door she hadn't seen before and she wondered how she could have missed it previously but gave a mental shrug. There was a soft beep and Paser lowered her arm to her side. To her astonishment, the identification pad began to slide back into the wall and disappeared from view. No wonder she'd hadn't seen it before. It was hidden by a panel.

"You now have access to the base to come and go as you please, but I would suggest you don't leave without one of us by your side." Paser gave her a heated look, reached for the door handle which hadn't been there before, and opened the door.

She followed him inside, acutely aware of Pen's eyes on her as they walked down the corridor. When she didn't hear the door close behind them, she looked back to see that it was shut tight, and although she tried to stop herself, she glanced up at Pen. Her breath caught in her throat when she saw that his gaze was locked on her ass, and even though she tried not to sway her hips more than they usually did when she walked naturally, she couldn't seem to help herself.

A low, rumbling groan was Pen's response and when he lifted his gaze to hers, she nearly stumbled. His eyes were so hungry and yet there was so much more than just lust in his gaze. If she could have named the emotion, she would have said it was love, but she knew she couldn't be right.

He had barely known her for twenty-four hours and there was no way he could have such feelings for her after such a short time.

She turned her head back to the front and gnawed on her bottom lip as a gamut of emotions raced through her heart and mind.

Uncertainty was the uppermost one because she had no idea what to do.

Ever since she was a little girl, she'd dreamt of her Prince Charming sweeping her off of her feet and spending the rest of their lives together, but she had never once envisaged meeting two men who could star in that role and wasn't sure if she was ready for that. In fact, she wasn't sure if she was ready for any of this.

She'd spent her entire life on the edge of society watching others find their dreams, only to have them turn to dust. Not once had she had someone hold her and tell her they loved her. If she took the huge step toward them and agreed to be with them, she didn't know if she would be able to pick up the pieces if they found her wanting.

And why wouldn't they?

No one else had ever found her worthy.

Chapter Five

Paser was so hungry for Nina he could barely think straight. After the kiss he'd shared with her, the need was so bad his legs were trembling and he felt like he was stumbling as he walked, but since Nina hadn't said anything he figured he didn't look awkward.

Since he had kissed her, he could feel a little of her emotions, but since she was going through every single feeling a person could, he wasn't sure what to do or say, but one thing was certain and that gave him hope. Hope that she would accept them as her mates, because he could feel her desire, and it was for him and Pen. The sweet, musky scent of her arousal permeated his nostrils every time he inhaled, and he wasn't sure if he should show her to their spare room and leave her to unpack her meagre possession alone or offer to help.

From the tension radiating from Pen, he was in just as much turmoil as Paser was. He followed his friend and mate into the spare bedroom of their apartment and sighed when she began to pull her belongings from the small, battered case. When she kept her back to him and Pen, he realized that she still needed time.

He sighed with frustration and ran his fingers through his hair. He felt like a real bastard because he was so eager for her to turn around and tell him that she was going to be with them forever, but they'd bombarded her with information and he was sure she probably felt like running instead of opening her arms and heart to them without question.

It was kind of funny for him to feel so much. Of course, he had feelings like every other living person, but after being alive and fighting for so long, he was sure at times that his heart was encased in ice. The moment he'd set eyes on Nina, the ice had melted and emotions had surged forth in a paroxysm of vehemence.

Paser hadn't been this unsure of himself since the moment Ra had appeared and saved their miserable hides. The confidence he'd built up over the years was taking a battering and he had no idea how to handle the insecurity he was feeling, but that was beside the point. What they needed to do was somehow engage Nina's heart and they needed to do it quickly. If she was being targeted by Apep and his demonic minions, the only way to really keep her safe was to mate with her.

He almost laughed at that. Yes, she was attracted to them, but he couldn't see her jumping into bed with him and Pen anytime soon. He tried to put himself in her shoes and drew in a deep breath when a shard of pain pierced his heart. The poor woman had been ripped out of her safe, secure world and thrust into a realm she probably never even imagined, even as a child. She had to be scared out of her mind after finding out that demons actually existed, let alone that she was being targeted by the underworld.

And then there was the fact that they had told her—or rather, Zara had—she was the mate to not one, but two demigods. No wonder he could feel a copious amount of tumult coming from her.

"Is there anything you need?" Paser asked, breaking the tension-filled silence.

"No, thank you." Nina replied so quietly that if he hadn't had such great hearing, he probably wouldn't have heard her. He glanced over at Pen and saw that he was frowning at Nina as if trying to figure her out, too. He nodded toward the door and began walking toward the exit.

"If you need anything, please don't hesitate to let us know."

Nina nodded but continued to try and ignore them. When he saw color rise in her cheeks, he knew she was as aware of them as they were of her, but decided to give her some time to gather herself and think about what she wanted.

"We'll be in the training room if you need us," Pen said.

"Okay," Nina answered.

Paser hurried out of their apartment and down the hall to the training room with Pen at his heels. No words were necessary, and they both grabbed a couple of swords from the wall and went at each other without restraint. They needed to get rid of the pent-up energy humming through their bodies.

The clash of metal on metal drowned out everything and after twenty minutes of sparring with swords, they dropped those and began hand-to-hand combat. They kicked, punched, ducked and spun in a parody of a violent dance until the fire burning in Paser's blood began to wane. It was only when they finally stopped that they noticed the other sentinels had entered the room.

"What's up with you two?" Set asked, but from the smirk on his face, their friend already knew the answer.

"Don't start," Pen snarled and shoved Set away.

"Where's Zara?" Paser asked.

"Right here," Zara replied.

Paser spun around to see Zara running flat out on the treadmill with the ease of a natural-born elite athlete. Since Set and Sab had claimed their mate, she had also become a demigod, and although she was still coming into her powers and learning her strengths, she could hold her own.

"Is Nina all right?" Zara asked.

"Yeah." Pen scrubbed a hand over his face and sighed before shaking his head. "I don't really know."

"She's just needs some time, Paser. She'll come around."

"Do you really believe that?" Pen asked.

"Yeah, I do. She'll try to resist you, but she won't be able to last long. If she feels anything like I did the first time I met Set and Sab, she's already half in love with you and her body will be craving your touch."

"I hope you're right, Zara," Pen said. "I don't know how much longer I can wait."

"You're kidding, right?" Mit smirked. "You've only just met her."

"Just you wait, Mitry Mosi." Zara pointed her finger at him. "When you meet your mate, I'm going to give you hell. You have no idea what it's like. The only way to describe what happens when you meet your mate, or mates in our case, is as if you're body goes into heat."

Mit snorted. "I have great control over my body. There is no way in hell I'm going to let a woman twist me up in knots."

"Famous last words, Mit. Just you wait."

Mit snorted and rolled his eyes. If it hadn't been for the lonely yearning in his friend's gaze, Paser would have risen to the other man's bait, but since he knew Mit was full of shit and pining for a mate of his own, he kept his mouth shut.

He walked over to the weights, and after loading it with weight plates, he began to lift and lower the bar. Usually he hoped that when they went out on demon patrol the night was quiet, but right now, he was itching for a fight and hoped like hell he could cut down a demon or two. Maybe then he wouldn't feel as if his skin was crawling with lust.

* * * *

Since she had so little, it didn't take Nina long to unpack her things, and now that she was done, she wasn't sure what to do. She was restless but needed time to come to terms with everything she'd learned. Sometimes she felt like she was caught up in the middle of a B-grade movie and wondered if she were dreaming, but there was no way she could have ever imagined such passionate kisses, and from two sexy, handsome men.

Sure, she'd dreamed of being kissed and made love to someday, but never would she have thought of having two men. However, since she'd met them and been told she was their mate, her imagination was in overdrive. She could imagine kissing one of them while the other caressed and made love to her body, and although she'd never thought of anal sex before now, it was becoming harder and harder to keep the images out of her head.

With a groan of frustration, Nina stopped pacing the room and wondered if Pen and Paser were still in the apartment. Although she wanted to look at them as often as possible, she didn't want to end up making a fool of herself by throwing herself at them. The yearning for their kisses and touches was getting more powerful with each passing second and she could have sworn she'd felt their disappointment before they left her be. How that was even possible, she had no idea, but figured she must have been hallucinating or something. Maybe she was going crazy after all. She knew if she told anyone what they had all told her, she would be no doubt trussed up into a strait jacket and locked in a padded room.

When she realized her thoughts were going around and around in circles, she pushed them aside and breathed in and out a few times, hoping to relieve the tension that had invaded her body, and then concentrated on tensing and relaxing each individual muscle. By the time she'd worked from her head to her toes, she was yawning and decided it wouldn't hurt to have a nap since she'd barely slept the night before.

She crawled onto the bed, pulled her knees up close to her chest and hugged the spare pillow. Before too long, she was drifting off to sleep.

The moment Nina became aware of her surroundings, fear skittered up her spine. The all-encompassing dark felt sinister with evil intent. She turned frantically, looking for any source of light to show her the way out, but there wasn't even a speck of illumination.

Her breathing escalated until she was taking shallow, noisy, rasping breaths and her heart was beating so hard all she could hear was her own blood whooshing in her ears. She held her breath, trying to listen for any noise, but she didn't hear anything. Sweat beaded on her brow and between her breasts, and her legs began to shake as fear took hold.

The air was thick and each time she drew in air, she felt as if her lungs were being clogged with thick, acrid smoke. Although she was cold because of her terror, she was also hot. Her skin was covered in a sheen of perspiration and she knew her fear was a semblance of reason for that reaction, but it was also because the air surrounding her felt as hot as she imagined Hades would be.

As that thought coalesced, terror tried to grab hold and if she could see where she was, she would have turned tail and ran, but how could she flee when she couldn't even see her own hand in front of her face?

Nina reached over and pinched her left arm with her right hand and bit her tongue to hold in the yelp of pain. She didn't want to alert anyone she was here because she had a feeling if she did, she would never get out, but she couldn't just stay here in the inky blackness for the rest of her life. She lifted both arms, placing her hands palm out in case she came up against a wall or some sort of obstruction, and took one step. When she didn't encounter anything in her path, she took another step and then another, shuffling her way along in the hope of finding a door or window she could escape through.

All of a sudden the hair on the back of her neck stood on end and her whole body quaked, but she couldn't let dread take over until she was a sniveling basket-case, so she took a breath of hot air and released it slowly. Her lungs burned and the rank stench of sulfur assailed her nose, nearly choking her with the rotten gas, but she was able to control her gag reflex. If by chance she wasn't alone, she didn't want to give whoever was in here with her the pleasure of showing the trepidation she was feeling.

Nina forced herself to keep moving slowly, determined to find her way out of the dark abyss, keeping her eyes wide open intent on finding a means of escape, but when she heard what sounded like the scrape of a boot on the ground and she shook so hard she could hear her teeth clacking together.

She must have blinked, because at first there was nothing but oily black everywhere she looked, and then, out of nowhere, two red dots appeared in the distance at least half a meter higher than her head. At first, she thought the dots were her way out, but when they disappeared for an infinitesimal moment before reappearing again, she began to back away.

The grating sound of evil laughter assaulted her ears like long fingernails being dragged down a blackboard, and she knew without a shadow of a doubt she was no longer alone. Horror slammed into her from every which way, and though she couldn't see, she wasn't staying. She spun on her heels and ran as she'd never run before in her life. Her arms and legs pumped up and down, adrenaline surging through her system to aid her flight. The raucous laughter sounded again and she whimpered when she felt a hot breeze against the back of her neck.

Her skin crawled with pain as if fiery talons had been raked over her flesh, and yet knew she hadn't been touched and thought that maybe she had indeed lost her mind. She grabbed hold of that thought and held on to it, deducing that her imagination was playing tricks on her after the stories she'd heard over the last twenty four hours.

She glanced back over her shoulder, and although she couldn't see the two red dots anymore, she kept right on running. That was until she slammed up against what felt like a brick wall. What little air she had left in her lungs whooshed out and she fell to her ass with her bruising thud. The inky blackness swirled around her seeming to thin out before her very eyes and mixed with wisps of red, lighting the area around her with a demonic glow.

That's when she saw him, standing off to the side with his arms crossed over his massive chest and a malicious smile on his face. As she stared at him in shock, she took in his handsome visage.

He was so big he was well over seven feet tall, and so muscular she was sure he'd put Hercules to shame. His hair was as black as night and reached his shoulders, but it didn't matter that he was good-looking. She could feel the evil radiating off of him. If she could have stopped herself from doing it, she would have, because when she looked into his bleak, malevolent eyes, she wondered if she was completely mad. In the depth of the soulless gaze was mayhem, torture and murder, and she was sure she heard the echo of screams.

When he took a step toward her, the ground beneath her ass vibrated and she whimpered with terror. She tried to pull her gaze from his, but no matter how hard she tried, she couldn't break the spell she was under. She must have moved her arms and didn't remember doing so, but was glad she had when her skin burned on the hot ground beneath her. The pain was enough to break the trance she'd been in and she was able to scuttle back on her hands and feet. A moan of despair escaped her mouth when her back connected with a hot rock wall. When she felt a tugging sensation in her chest she looked down.

A cry of pain left her mouth as agony seared her chest. It felt like someone was trying to rip her heart out. Two handsome faces appeared in her mind's eye and she wished she could touch them one more time. She hadn't even realized how important Pen and Paser had become to her in such a short amount of time, until her life was in jeopardy. Now that she'd probably never see them again, everything seemed to come to her with such clarity and she would give anything to spend just one more second with them.

That was the moment Nina realized she'd virtually given up, and renewed determination filled her soul. If she wanted to have a chance to be with Pentu and Paser, she needed to fight for them.

She envisioned their faces and the emotions that had been in their eyes when they looked at her, and gasped with recognition. The love they had for her had been evident if she'd only cared to look. It didn't matter that they'd only just met. It was like she'd been hit with a bolt of lightning. They were meant to be together and she wasn't about to let some evil guy take away her chances of being loved.

For the first time in her life, Nina let the walls around her heart drop, and when she did, the emptiness in her heart filled with warmth. To her surprise, the inky black-and-red fog began to dissipate and her surroundings began to lighten. She looked back up to where the giant, handsome man with eerie red eyes had been, only to discover he wasn't there.

The tugging at her chest lessened, as did the pain, and her body jolted as hope filled her heart.

For the first time in her life, Nina felt as if she was lovable just like anyone else, and her childhood dreams came back to the fore. She didn't care that they all still had a lot to learn about each other. All that mattered was that she open herself up to the possibility of love instead of hiding behind the walls she'd erected at a young age. From what she'd been told, they had a very long time to learn about each other, and what better way to do that than if she mated with them?

Her trepidation was unwarranted, from what Zara had told her, and once she was mated with Pen and Paser, they would do everything in their power to protect her and make her happy. She wasn't sure she was in love with them yet, but she definitely had strong feelings for them and she'd be a fool to turn her back on something that could end up being something special.

She'd let her fears of being hurt rule her for so long it had become a habit. It was going to be hard to keep an open mind and heart, but she needed to see where this thing between her, Paser and Pen could go.

The epiphany was enough to jolt her back to wakefulness, and the moment she opened her eyes, it was to see Pen and Paser each holding one of her hands and stroking her arm.

"Are you all right, baby?" Pen asked, a frown of concern marring his face.

"Yes," she answered, mentally cursing when her voice cracked.

"Are you sure, sweetheart?" Paser brushed a strand of hair back from her face.

"I think so," she replied, and then to her horror she burst into tears.

The last twenty-four hours or so had finally caught up with her and she couldn't keep the emotional storm that had been building from bursting free.

Pen lifted her from the bed, plonked her in his lap and surrounded her with his arms and body heat. The tears flowed hard and fast, and no matter how much she tried to stop them, it was impossible. She cried so much her eyes became sore and puffy, and she had trouble drawing air into her lungs.

Paser moved in behind her, pressing his front to her back, and for the first time since she'd fallen asleep, she felt safe and cherished. It took a while, but finally her tears stopped, her neck occasionally spasming with each hiccupped breath she drew in.

"You were screaming, Nina. Did you have a nightmare?" Pen kissed the top of her head and she nodded as she snuggled into him.

"Do you want to talk about it, sweetheart?" Paser began to knead the tense muscles in her neck.

"Have you ever seen Apep?" Nina felt both men tense at her question and she couldn't help do the same. She wasn't sure she wanted an answer to her question, but she couldn't go around with her head buried in the sand. She wasn't so sure her nightmare had actually been a nightmare and there was only one way to find out.

"No. Why do you ask?" Paser began kneading her muscles again.

"I think I may know what he looks like."

"What?" Pen shouted his question. He leaned back slightly and cupped her face in his palm. "Look at me, Nina."

She couldn't deny his command, and while her eyes and nose were no doubt red and her face blotchy, she found herself obeying him. He stared deeply into her eyes and she shivered in reaction to what she saw in their depths. There was lust and love, but the most prominent emotion she could see was concern. "Tell us what happened."

Nina cleared her croaky throat and then told them about her nightmare.

"Fuck! I don't like this." Paser rose from the bed and began to pace. "Apep and his demons don't usually attack during the day."

"So you think this was an attack on me?" Nina shivered with fear.

"Yes." Pen's voice drew her gaze. He was grinding his teeth so hard the muscle in his jaw was twitching.

"You know what worries me?" Paser asked as he looked at Pen.

"What?" Nina asked, but both of the men remained silent. She knew then that they were hiding something from her but she wasn't about to let them. If she was going to be their mate and help them fight evil, she needed to know everything she could so she was better prepared if she ever came face-to-face with Apep and his demons again.

She shoved Pen's arms from around her, scrambled from his lap and from the bed before planting her feet on the floor, hands on hips as she faced them.

"You need to tell me." She glared at them for good measure, hoping that they would see things her way. Although she knew they were keeping their thoughts to themselves to protect her, information was the key. She needed to know anything and everything she could so that next time she faced the god of the underworld, she would be confident in her fight.

Pen sighed and nodded at Paser before meeting her gaze. "Apep never does his own dirty work. He always sends one of his peons to do it for him."

"And?" Nina asked, because she knew there was more.

"From what we've learned over the years, Apep has never appeared in any of the nightmares."

"So you've just said twice." Nina relaxed her stance and sighed. "What aren't you telling me?"

"Apep was sent to the bowels of hell and has been trying to escape for millennia." Paser grimaced as he crossed his arms over his chest.

"You've already told me this. Well, Zara did, anyway."

"What Zara didn't tell, because she probably doesn't know, is the reason Apep has never materialized in the dreams or tried to steal souls himself, is because he was never strong enough," Pen explained.

Nina gasped and covered her mouth with her hand. Once more fear tried to swamp her as frissons of alarm raced up her spine, sending goosebumps of horror over her skin.

If Apep was now able to infiltrate dreams and during the day, did that mean he was nearly strong enough to escape from the underworld?

Chapter Six

Pen wanted to run to Ra's temple and seek out the sun god, but from the horrified expression on Nina's face and the way she started to shake, she needed him and Paser more than ever. He hadn't felt fear in so long, and now that it was surging through his system he wasn't quite sure how to handle it. He wanted to hunt down the demonic and wipe them from the face of the earth and the underworld, as well as their evil ruler, but he couldn't.

He had often wanted to ask Ra why he didn't just go into the underworld and slaughter the evil, but he wasn't sure the sun god would ever answer him, so he'd kept his mouth shut. However, now that he'd met his mate and she was in danger, he wanted to rage at all of them for the continuous struggle over good versus evil.

Pen shoved to his feet, clasped Nina by her shoulders and pulled her against his body. She wrapped her arms around his waist and hugged him tight.

"Am I going to die?"

Her whispered question tore his heart in two and for the first time since he was a young boy, tears burned the back of his eyes. "No. We won't let them get you, baby. Paser and I will do everything within our power to keep you safe. I would give my own life before any harm came to you."

"Don't say that." Nina drew back and met his gaze.

He hated seeing the tears in her eyes and fear in their depths, but until the threat of Apep and his demon shadows were no longer, there was nothing he could do to wipe it away.

"Why didn't we feel the surge of evil like we normally do?" Paser asked the question that had been in Pen's mind ever since Nina had told them about the attack.

"I don't know."

"What are you talking about?" Nina asked.

"Usually we can sense evil and are drawn to it, but we didn't this time." Pen hugged her tighter, but made sure not to squeeze too hard in case he hurt her.

"What does it feel like?"

"It's dark, thick and oily. Almost like what you'd imagine sludge would feel like, but it's also hot and oppressive, making it difficult to breathe," Paser explained.

"That's exactly how it felt to me." Nina nodded. "How do you deal with that night after night and remain sane?"

"It was hard at first," Pen said, "but after dealing with the demonic for thousands of years, you train yourself to become immune to the affects. In a way, I suppose we numb ourselves to the sensation."

"Do the others feel the same things you do?" Nina moved from Pen's arms and sat on the edge of the bed.

"Yeah, I think so." Pen crossed his arms.

"How could you not know?" she asked with a frown.

"We used to talk about it all the time when we first became sentinels making sure we all felt it so we could follow and fight evil, but I guess we've become a little complacent and just stopped talking about it anymore." Paser frowned as if thinking about what he'd just said.

"Do you think you could have become immune to the sensations?"

"We still feel evil whenever it's prevalent, but I suppose we could be more invulnerable after fighting for so long," Pen admitted.

"Why would I be targeted?" Nina asked.

Pen cleared his throat and glanced at Paser.

"Didn't Zara explain about the demons targeting the innocent?" Paser asked.

"Yes, but she also said that the demonic could be acquiring their army through the not-so-innocent."

"Yes, but the more pure the innocent the person's soul is, the stronger the shadow demon will be." Pen sat down beside Nina.

She frowned at him and then Paser before meeting his gaze again. "Are you telling me the only reason I've been targeted is because I'm a virgin?"

Pen felt his cheeks heat, and he wanted to look away from her intent gaze but didn't. "No, baby. An innocent doesn't have to be a virgin."

"What? That doesn't make sense. If a person has lost their virginity then they're no longer innocent."

"Not necessarily, sweetheart." Paser knelt on the floor and placed his hands on Nina's thighs.

Pen wanted to strip her down and make love to her, but talking to her was more important than his physical needs. Plus, she hadn't gifted him or Paser with her acceptance yet and until she did, they needed to keep tight reign over their lust.

"What do you mean by that?"

"Just because a person has had sex doesn't mean they're not innocent anymore. The term innocent can be used in relation to a person's heart and soul. It's what's inside that matters."

"So why me? Besides the virgin bit."

"You radiate goodness, Nina. Your soul is so pure, and you practically glow with it."

Nina snorted, but when she met Pen's eyes, he made sure she knew he was being sincere and not just feeding her a line.

"Pen's right, sweetheart. You are the epitome of pure and good, but not because of your sexual experience or lack thereof."

"How can you say that? You don't even know me," Nina said.

"Have you ever deliberately gone out of your way to hurt anyone?" Paser asked.

Nina sighed with what sounded like exasperation. "No."

"I'll bet the exact opposite is true," Pen said.

"Besides working in a bar, what did you spend your free time doing, Nina?"

"Reading, listening to music, watching movies and TV."

"And?" Paser raised his eyebrow.

"Helping out in the local shelter," she murmured.

"I'll bet that's not all, is it?" Pen asked.

Nina shook her head.

"What else?" Paser questioned.

"I used to visit the elderly in the retirement homes," she mumbled.

"And?" Pen raised an eyebrow knowing there was more she wasn't telling.

"I sat with babies in the hospital and held them when their parents couldn't."

"You see." Paser wrapped an arm around her shoulders and pulled her closer to his side. "We know how good you are on the inside."

"What has that got to do with anything?"

"Everything." Pen waved his hand in the air. "You missed out on all those things when you were growing up, didn't you?"

She didn't answer verbally but bit her lip. Pen could see the moisture gathering in her eyes and his heart ached for her. She had had no one to love and care for her and although she had managed to keep herself apart from other people because she was scared to open herself up and get even more hurt, she hadn't kept herself from showering love on others.

Pen cupped her face between her hands and stared earnestly into the depths of her eyes. He swore he could see an aura of pure white light shining from within her very essence. "You are the most loving, giving person I have ever had the fortune to meet. If only more people were like you, there wouldn't be such segregation between the classes.

No one would ever go hungry or be without clothes, and not have roofs over their heads."

"I'm no one special." Nina glanced to the side before meeting his gaze again. "I don't even know who my parents were."

"That is neither here nor there, baby." Pen swallowed around the lump of emotion constricting his throat. "It doesn't matter where you came from. What matters is what you do with your life, and you, Nina Page, should be held up in the highest esteem."

"Now you're just mocking me."

Pen hated that she was refuting his statement. "How many other people do you know who would have done the things you have?"

"There are a lot of people who give freely of their time to help others in need."

"That may be." Paser gave her a squeeze. "But we aren't concerned with anyone but you."

"I already have feelings for you, Nina. I care for you more than I have ever cared about another living soul," Pen put as much sincerity in his voice as he could. He needed her to understand how much she meant to him even if she wasn't ready to hear he loved her.

"But how can you? We've known each other for barely more than a few hours."

"I care for you, too, sweetheart." Paser stroked a finger down a cheek. "Do you think we wouldn't know how we feel about someone when we've lived for so long? We were both attracted to you from the moment we set eyes on you. We know the difference between lust and l…caring."

"Paser's right." Pen brushed a strand of hair, which had fallen over her eye, away and nearly smiled when she shivered in reaction. He knew they were getting through to her because he could see the yearning in her eyes every time she looked at them, but Nina was a very deep person. She needed to know that what they had between them was more than desire.

"There's a connection between us, baby, and not just mutual attraction, although that does play a large part in a relationship in the beginning. If the lust is mutual there is usually a spark of physical attraction, but with you there is so much more."

Pen placed his hand over his heart and drew a deep breath. He knew his next words would either make or break their relationship. If she didn't believe him, she would continue to keep them at an arm's length and maybe even walk away from them when all this was over. It would kill him if she did, but if that was what she wanted, they would have to let her go. However, he wasn't going to go down without a fight. He was used to fighting, but this fight was the most important one of their lives and he wasn't giving up.

"Don't you feel anything for us, Nina?"

She sighed and nodded her head, still gnawing on her lip. Pen wanted to lean in and lick the tortured flesh, but he and Paser needed to convince her to mate with them first. When she agreed to accept them as being theirs, her men, her mates, then he would kiss, soothe and arouse every inch of her beautiful, precious body.

"Tell us the reason for your hesitation, sweetheart," Paser encouraged.

"What if you find me lacking? What if once we're mated, you realize you don't like me? You'd be saddled with a woman you didn't love and would end up resenting me. If I allowed myself to care for you and you walked away, I would end up getting hurt."

"That won't ever happen, baby." Pen wiped at the tear that leaked from her eye. "We already have feelings for you. We know our own minds and hearts, Nina. We will *never* leave you."

"Relationships aren't always smooth sailing," she said quietly. "We are sure to fight. What then?"

"Everyone fights, sweetheart. No one person is perfect."

"I know," she wailed. "I'm not either. You've both got me up on a pedestal and when I fall off, you're not going to like what you see."

"This is getting us nowhere," Pen snapped with frustration.

"See, you're already getting annoyed with me."

"So what?" Pen stood and flung his hands up with exasperation. "I'm only human."

"But you're not," Nina cried. "You're demigods."

The moment she said those words, it was like a light bulb had gone off. She was scared she wouldn't measure up to them because they were Ra's sentinels and more than human.

"What has that got do with anything?" Paser asked in a growly voice.

"Everything." Nina rose to her feet and began pacing. "I have no idea what I'm supposed to do. Zara told me that if I agreed to be your mate, I would end up like you. What if I stuff up and anger the sun god? Will he come down from the heavens and smite me until there is nothing left? I don't know the first thing about worshipping a deity. I've never even been to church."

"Neither have we," Pen said with a sigh.

Nina turned and looked at him incredulously. "Are you serious?"

"Very. I have never lied to you and I never will. Ra appointed us his sentinels because we were the only slaves to save an elderly man from being beaten to death. He saw something in us that he liked and that was that." Pen ran his fingers through his hair.

"We aren't saints, sweetheart," Paser moved closer and clasped her hand. "We've been with women over the centuries. We've made mistakes."

"You have?"

"Yeah, we have," Pen replied.

"Like what?"

"We've lost people to the shadow demons because we couldn't get a lock on the demonic's location and weren't in time to save the innocents." Paser rubbed his thumb over the back of her hand.

"But you tried," she whispered.

"Yes."

"That's all any of us can do, baby. We try to do our best and if we fail, we can't beat ourselves up over that failure. All anyone can do is be themselves and do the best they can." Pen cupped her face, leaned in and kissed her on the forehead.

"Ra will never ask you to do anything beyond your ability. If you agree to be our mate, it's going to take time for your powers to kick in, to grow in strength. No one expects you to go out and fight alongside us if you don't wish to, including us."

"And if I want to?"

Paser moved in behind her and wrapped his arms around her waist. "Then we will train you so that you can fight by our sides."

"You would do that? Really? You would teach me how to fight?"

"If that's what you want, yes," Pen answered emphatically.

"Thank you." Nina smiled.

He was stunned by her beauty. She glowed from the inside out and when he met her gaze, he felt like he was drowning in her amazing blue orbs. His body reacted to her scent and her proximity. His cock, which had been half hard or at full attention since he'd met Nina, twitched and filled with blood. He licked his lips and stared at her mouth. The urge to lean down and kiss her was almost too intense to ignore.

Pen didn't even realize he was gasping for breath as hunger surged through his veins until his head began to swim. He needed to claim his mate more than anything else in the world right now, but until he and Paser had her permission to do so, he was scared to touch her. He was worried her would lose control and take what hadn't been freely given, and if that happened, he knew she would end up hating him, and rightly so.

Pen had never felt this way in his long, lonely existence and knew he never would again. Nina was his mate and the only woman he wanted, would ever want now that they'd met. Every other woman before her paled in comparison and he knew no other would measure up to her if she denied them.

He wanted to beg her to say yes. He would even get down on his knees if he thought that would sway her, but he knew it wouldn't. It was her decision to make. He would be devastated if she refused them, but he would have to find a way to live with her decision.

Even if it ended up killing him.

Chapter Seven

Until she'd voiced her concerns about mating with Pen and Paser, Nina hadn't really understood why she was hesitating. She knew that they both believed every word they'd said, and although it humbled her at how they saw her, she wasn't perfect by any stretch of the imagination.

She felt as if a load had been lifted from her shoulders when they told her that there were no expectations on her if she agreed to be their mate. The worry over stuffing up or insulting their sun god had been a like a thorn in her side she hadn't known was there until she'd brushed up against something. Now that they'd appeased her worries, she felt as if she could take the next step. She was more than just attracted to the two men, and from what they'd said, they were, too. Her feelings for them had grown stronger with each minute they spent together and her body had been in a near-constant ache to have their touch.

There really was no reason to deny being their mate anymore. They had cleared up her uncertainties and she was eager to take the next step.

She took several deep breaths, trying to calm her racing heart. She was nervous as hell because she had never been with a man before and she was about to get two. They were also very big, and from the hard ridges she'd felt against her body a couple of times, they were well in proportion in the penis department to the rest of their big, muscular frames.

However, while she'd been cautious about who she let into her heart, she was more than eager to have them make love to her, even if she was a little trepidatious. She knew from their words and actions so far that they would never hurt her physically or emotionally on purpose.

She met Paser's gaze and saw dejection in his eyes, and realized that she had put the look there. She'd hurt him and Pen with her distrust and hesitation, and though she hated what she'd done, it had been necessary for her to understand everything.

They were also right. No one was infallible. No one person could claim absolute perfection or sin-free lives. Humans by nature made mistakes. The only travesty with that was if the lessons learned were ignored.

Plus, this could be her only chance at ever finding love and she had a feeling that the emotions roiling around inside her for the two men would only grow stronger.

She didn't want to have to look back over her life and have regrets. The choices she'd made in her life had been done with cold, analytical calculation that hadn't engaged her heart except when she had been holding those small, precious babies in her arms. Her heart had been fully on board with those beautiful little bundles of joy.

She could continue to go through life looking in from the outside, always being lonely and never feeling much of anything, or she could grab hold of what was on offer and maybe find happiness for the first time in her life.

She wouldn't know unless she chose to take a risk. Wasn't life one big risk after another?

"Yes."

"What?" Pen's sad eyes lit up with hope as he stared at her.

She glanced at Paser to see he was looking at her the same way.

"Yes, what?" Paser asked in a hoarse voice.

"I want to be your mate."

The disappointment and dejection left their eyes completely. Slow smiles spread across their faces, transforming their stern visages to joyous handsomeness.

Pen locked gazes with her and clasped her upper arms. "Are you sure, Nina? Once we mate with you, there will be no going back."

"We won't ever let you go," Paser declared.

"I'm sure."

"Thank the gods," Pen rasped right before his mouth slanted over hers.

Nina clutched at his shirt as his lips moved over hers and his tongue pressed in to rub against her own. She sighed into his mouth, loving his spicy, manly taste and savoring his flavor on her taste buds.

When Paser began to lick and nibble on the skin of her neck, she moaned and tried to get closer to both the men, but no matter how hard she tried, she couldn't seem to get close enough.

A whimper escaped her mouth when Paser nipped at her earlobe and then sucked on the skin beneath her ear. She shivered as the liquid desire in her belly grew warmer and began to spread to every extremity she had.

Pen twirled his tongue around hers and then sucked on her tip, causing her wet pussy to clench and release more cream onto her already-damp panties. She shifted on her feet and gasped when her belly brushed against Pen's hard cock, and without conscious thought began to rock her hips.

She groaned with disappointment when Pen broke the kiss and didn't even realize her fingers were tangled up in the cotton of his shirt until he pried them loose.

"I need you, baby. So damn much," Pen's voice was hoarse with desire.

"I need you, too. Both of you."

"And you shall have us, sweetheart." Paser swept her from her feet and moved toward the bed. He gently lowered her to the mattress and then his fingers were on the hem of her shirt. He pushed the material up, exposing her lower belly. The brush of his fingers on her heated skin made the muscles on her abs twitch.

"You are so fucking soft." Paser groaned and then he lowered his head, licking across her stomach, leaving a wet trail which caused goosebumps in his wake as the air in the room cooled her heated, damp flesh. Paser lifted his head, gave her a gentle smile and then pulled her shirt up over her head. When his eyes snagged on her bra-clad breasts, her first instinct was to cover her nakedness, but she held still and let him look. If they were going to be her mates, she would need to get used to being naked in front of them.

"Abso-fucking-lutely gorgeous." Pen growled, drawing her gaze.

Nina's breath hitched in her throat when she looked at Pen. While Paser had been kissing her belly, he'd taken the time to remove his clothes.

He had wide, muscular shoulders, defined pecs, bulging biceps and a narrow waist. The hair between his pecs made her fingers tingle and she wanted to know whether it was as soft as the hair on his head or coarser, and she would find out soon enough. She let her eyes wander down over his thick, brawny thighs before taking a deep breath and gazing at his groin. Her heart flipped over when she caught sight of his long, thick cock and she licked her dry lips.

"Lie down, sweetheart." Paser gently pushed on her shoulder and she obeyed his directive without a qualm. He got up onto the bed beside her and pressed his lips to hers.

Nina smoothed her hands over his shoulders, the back of his neck, and threaded her fingers into his hair. He tasted different, but just as good as Pen did, and she never wanted them to stop kissing her. No matter how many times their lips met hers, she knew she would never get enough. She wanted to crawl in under their skin and worm her way into their hearts, like they had already done to hers.

She felt the bed dip near her feet and then the button on her jeans was tugged open, before they were pulled down over her hips and away. Goose bumps raced over her skin and she shivered, but not because she was cold. The total opposite was the reason she was trembling. Her whole body was on fire.

"Please," she whispered against Paser's lips.

"We will, sweetheart." Paser kissed over her shoulder down her arm, and then over the top of her breasts. She didn't even notice he'd unclipped her bra until she felt the straps sliding down her arms.

She startled when large, warm, manly hands smoothed up and down her shins, getting higher and higher with each pass until the tips of Pen's fingers brushed against the edge of her panties.

"I can smell you, baby. You smell so fucking sweet." Pen kissed her hip before laving the tip of his tongue over the flesh-covered bone. A giggle escaped before she could stop it, but it didn't seem to bother him any.

She held her breath when Pen's thumbs hooked into the waist of her panties and slowly pulled them down. The air left her lungs in a gasp when Paser cupped a breast in his hand and licked over the hard peak.

Her eyes fluttered closed and she arched her chest to get more of the exquisite sensations humming through her body. When Pen's hand cupped her naked mound, she cried out in shocked pleasure. She hadn't been expecting him to do that, but now that he was, she wanted more. He didn't press hard, but the slight pressure on her wet cunt caused her clit to throb and cream dripped from her hole.

"I can feel you," Pen gasped as he maneuvered between her legs. "I can feel how much you want us. Your little clit is throbbing right along with your heart."

"Please?" Nina begged and then looked down to meet Pen's heated green eyes. She stared at him in awe when she saw fangs protruding from his mouth.

"Don't be afraid of me, baby. I won't ever hurt you."

"I'm not afraid."

"That's good," Paser said, and when she turned to him, she saw his fangs had also elongated. He winked at her and then dipped his head to her chest. He blew over her nipple, hardening it even more, and then he sucked the peak into his mouth.

A long, low moan escaped her parted lips when Pen ran his finger up through her wet folds and rubbed lightly over her clit. The internal muscles in her cunt clenched reflexively and she bowed her hips up.

Pen wrapped his arms around her upper thighs and as he spread her legs wider, he bent his head closer to her pussy. He breathed in deeply, audibly, and then growled in approval right before he licked her pussy from top to bottom and back again.

"Oh," Nina groaned, her lower belly spasming and her legs shaking.

Paser released her nipple and met her gaze. "Do you like that, sweetheart? Do you like the way Pen is licking your pretty, little, virgin cunt?"

"God! Yes!"

Paser threaded his fingers through her hair, slammed his mouth over hers, and kissed her voraciously.

Nina whimpered and moaned but kissed him back just as hungrily. Each time Pen swiped his tongue over her pussy, the muscles in her body grew tauter. She felt as if she was a boiler or pressure cooker that was about to explode.

Paser broke the kiss, cupped one breast in his hand and began to knead it while he licked, sucked and scraped his teeth over the other nipple, being careful not to nick her with his fangs.

The more they kissed, touched and stroked her, the more she felt, and not just the physical element of things. She could feel waves of desire pouring off of Pentu and Paser, and fleetingly wondered how that was even possible, but then all thoughts scattered to the wind.

Pen rimmed her vagina with the tip of a finger and then slowly pushed it up inside. Nina panted and moaned at the foreign-yet-highly-pleasurable sensation and arched her hips up toward him, trying to get his finger further inside of her aching, wet pussy.

"Easy, sweetheart," Paser mumbled against her breast. "Let Pen prepare you."

"I'm ready. Now!" she declared in a near shout.

The ache in her womb was more intense than ever and she knew only her mates could ease the lustful pain.

"Just let me…" Pen murmured as he stroked his finger in and out of her pussy, causing her to moan as the heat inside grew to unbearable levels.

A light coat of perspiration beaded her skin, and yet she was covered in goose bumps and shivering uncontrollably. Pen added another finger to her pussy and he spread them apart, stretching her untried muscles as he pumped them in and out of her sheath.

The more he delved into her cunt, the tauter her muscles became. His fingers, sliding along her internal walls, were creating the most excruciating pleasure she'd ever felt in her life. She could feel the pressure inside building higher and higher and wondered if the top of her head would explode.

The tip of Pen's tongue swirled around and laved over her clit, and that only seemed to add to the molten sensations coursing through her veins, and then all of a sudden she was on the cusp of something so big, she wasn't sure she'd survive it.

She opened her mouth to tell them to stop but nothing came out. A long, low keening sound assailed her ears when Pen flicked the tip of his tongue rapidly over her throbbing clit, and then she went flying.

Nina flew so high she couldn't see the ground. White lights flashed before her eyes as she went hurtling up into the stratosphere, past the twinkling stars and into the heavens. Her pussy clenched and released, as the fire culminated into a crescendo so hot she wondered if she'd be burned alive. Her body shook and shivered as wave after wave of rapture tossed her about in a sea of nirvana. Cream gushed from her cunt and she thrashed about in the throes of ecstasy.

She had no idea how long the climax lasted. It could have been minutes, hours or days, but when she came back to herself, it was to find that Paser had moved off the bed and Pen was blanketing her body and holding her face between his hands.

"I–I…"

"Shh, baby. I know." Pen dipped his head and kissed her. She clung to his shoulders and kissed him back, pushing everything she felt toward him, hoping he would understand what she was saying with her body.

She lifted her legs, wrapped them around his waist and gasped when his hard cock brushed against her sensitive clit, but she was determined to have him and Paser for her mates and didn't want to wait any longer. She wriggled her hips until the head of his dick was aligned with her cunt and arched up, taking the tip inside of her.

"Fuck!" Pen growled and gasped, pressing his forehead against hers. "You feel so damn good, baby. Hot. Wet. Tight."

"More," Nina demanded, her pussy clenched around his corona, trying to pull him further inside of her.

"Wait!" Pen gasped, but then he moaned when her pussy clenched on him again.

Nina couldn't wait another minute. She removed her legs from around his waist, planted her feet on the mattress and then levered her hips up into his, taking as much of his erection into her cunt as she could.

Her muscles were tighter than she expected and she felt a slight burning pain as they adjusted to having his thick cock straining against her walls, but there was no real pain, thankfully.

"Damn it, baby. I didn't want to hurt you."

"You didn't. You aren't."

Pen lifted up onto his elbows to meet her gaze. "Are you sure, Nina?"

"Yes. You feel so good."

"As do you, mate. As do you."

Pen lowered his mouth to hers and kissed her with all the hunger she felt, and she kissed him right back. She gasped when he withdrew until the tip of his cock was still resting inside of her, and she was about to wrap her legs back around his hips and pull him back in, but he beat her to it.

He surged inside her in a long, slow, gentle stroke, the bulbous head of his hard dick massaging along the internal walls of her wet cunt, drawing out a low moan from deep inside her chest.

"Oh, so good. Pen, I want you."

"You've got me, baby. For the rest of our lives."

"Yes."

Nina gave herself up to the ecstatic pleasure of having Pen make love to her. He rocked his hips back and forth, his cock sliding in and out of her pussy. Each time he drove into her, he sped up and pushed in deeper, harder.

She caressed her hands over his shoulders, down her back and toward his muscular ass, but he was so much bigger and taller than she was that she could only reach his lower back. She groaned with frustration at her lack of reach.

Pen kissed her hard on the mouth and then pushed up until he was on his knees between her splayed thighs, gripping her hips and lifting them from the bed so that his hard penis remained inside of her cunt. He shuffled down the bed until her ass was on the edge of the mattress and he lowered his feet to the floor. He bent over her and kissed her again before releasing her mouth, pushed his hands beneath her ass, gripped her cheeks and lifted her even higher.

She had no idea where Paser had been but she noticed he was naked as he got back onto the bed beside her. Her gaze wandered over his delectable, muscular frame and her arousal grew even hotter. He was a little more muscular than Pen, but he was just as handsome and made her engine rev as much as Pen did.

Paser rested on his side, cupped a breast while strumming his thumb over the peak and kissed her rapaciously.

Nina was so overwhelmed with sensations and emotions she couldn't separate what she was feeling, but gave up when Pen began to fuck her hard, fast and deep.

His cock was hot and heavy inside of her, but amazingly pleasurable. Each time he shoved in deep and withdrew, the friction inside built up higher and higher.

Paser released her lips, scraped his teeth over her nipple and then suckled on it firmly. Nina cried out as another wave of sensation wracked her body, making her quake.

"Come on, Nina. Come for me, baby."

"I can't," Nina gasped, her head moving back and forth on the mattress as she panted for breath.

"Yes, you can, sweetheart. Let go."

"I'm trying," she wailed as she reached for the elusive pinnacle, but it remained out of her grasp.

"Move, Paser," Pen ordered in a harsh tone.

Nina wondered what was happening but had her answer a moment later when Pen covered her body with his. He pounded her into the mattress, his hard cock shuttling in and out of her cunt, hard, fast and deep. Each time his pelvis connected with hers, he gave a little twist of his hips, which brought his pubis in contact with her clit, sending her up even higher.

He scraped his fangs down her neck, causing her to tremble and moan, and just as she hovered on the precipice, his teeth sank into her flesh.

Nina cried out. Her cunt clamped down hard around his still-gliding cock before releasing only do to so again, and again. Flashes exploded before her eyes and she shook and shivered in unremitting convulsions of nirvanic bliss. Juices dripped from her pussy, covering Pen's dick, her inner thighs and finally her ass.

The flashes of light ceased and darkness beaconed as the carnal gratification consumed her. She hovered on the edge of hedonistic decadent completion for what seemed like forever before she started to come back from the earth shattering high in time to hear Pen shout as he, too, reached climax. Her cunt pulsed with aftershocks each time his cock jerked as he poured his seed deep into her womb, before collapsing on top of her. Their heavy panting was loud in the quiet after the carnal storm, and yet she felt more grounded than she'd ever been in her life.

Every part of her body was hyper sensitive and hyper aware of every place their bodies touched, especially where they were still joined, but that wasn't all. Nina felt connected to Pen on such a deep level she thought she might be imagining it at first.

For some unknown reason, she turned her mind inward and tuned into her soul. She found the inner light that wasn't hers and followed it back to Pen. Tears formed in her eyes, welled and then flowed over her cheeks. She had no idea how it was possible, and though Zara had told her about the bond that she would have to Pen and Paser if she agreed to be their mate, she hadn't really believed her. She couldn't do so now. She was inside of Pen's heart and she could feel his joy that she had accepted him and Paser, and she could feel his love.

Love so poignant and profound it hurt, but it was all for her.

Chapter Eight

Paser had never been so happy in his life. When Nina had agreed to be their mate, he'd wanted to shout with joy, but he hadn't wanted to startle her. The hardest thing he'd ever had to do was let her and Pen have their moment as they made love and mated. He wanted to love Nina like he'd never loved any other woman.

She was so damn special, beautiful inside and out, and had no idea how gorgeous she was. That in itself was appealing. Most of the women he and Pen had been with knew how to use their bodies to get what they wanted, and while he didn't condemn them for it, now they seemed so jaded, so cynical. Nina's heart and soul were as pure as the flakes of a fresh snowfall and he wanted to bask in her purity.

Pen kissed her deeply and then rolled off of her, stood, winked and grinned at him, and then strode toward the bathroom.

Paser wanted to tug Nina into his arms, but he refrained. He was nervous about mating with Nina, which was absolutely ludicrous since he'd been with and satisfied countless women, but she wasn't just any woman. Nina was his mate and special. He wanted everything to be absolutely perfect for her, but he was worried that he would become too eager and hurt her. He was so famished for her he was trembling. He took a deep breath and released it slowly before he rolled closer to her and caressed her arm.

He bit his lip when she shivered, and to his surprise, she became the instigator. She rolled over before scrambling up onto her hands and knees, lifted a leg and straddled him.

"Are you okay?" She frowned down at him.

"Yes. Why?"

"You look…I don't know, kind of worried."

Paser decided that honesty was the best policy. "I don't want to hurt you."

"What makes you think you will?"

He lifted a hand and let her see how pent-up he was. "I'm shaking."

Nina grinned, plopped her ass on his stomach and lifted her own hand. "So am I."

"Come here, sweetheart." The moment his hands gripped her hips, all his worries ceased. Just having her skin beneath his was enough to steady him.

She leaned down and brushed her lips over his. He groaned, threaded his fingers into her short just to the shoulders black hair and devoured her mouth. She responded without hesitation and he set about building her desire so he could make love with and claim her as his very own. Her tongue stroked around and along his, causing the embers to flare deep in his gut.

His cock twitched and jerked as pre-cum bubbled to the surface. Nina broke the kiss before licking and nibbling her way down his neck, and when she scraped her teeth over the tendon, he nearly shot off the bed.

"Hmm," she hummed against his skin before doing it again and again. His cock throbbed and pulsed each time his heart beat and he swore it had never been so hard. He loved having her mouth on him and her hands were caressing over his shoulders, chest, and finally his upper torso. He wished she wasn't sitting on his belly so she could grip his cock and stroke him, but he was just happy to have her touch. The emotions pouring off of her were becoming more intense with each second that passed, and he couldn't wait to give her the claiming bite so that they would be connected on a deeper emotional level.

He held his breath when she wiggled further down his legs and groaned as she licked over the abs outlined in his stomach. Each touch was better than the last, and she was setting his blood and body on fire. He wanted to reach down grab her arms, haul her up over him and sink his cock in her wet pussy, but he also wanted her mouth on him. His mind was conflicted, but his body knew exactly what he wanted because he remained still and gasped for breath.

A low, rumbling growl formed deep in his chest and out of his parted lips when she pressed her nose to the base of his cock and inhaled. He looked down and nearly came when he saw the way she was studying his dick so intently. He'd never seen anything so sexily carnal and right in his life. She was his and he was hers, and he wasn't sure he could hold out much longer. A fine trembling had started in his legs and was moving up into his body and arms. He was so fucking hungry for her that the primal need surging through him was almost painful.

He gasped with pleasure-pain as she wrapped her small hand around his dick and lifted it toward her mouth. The moment her moist, pink little tongue swiped over the head was the moment he lost it.

Paser didn't even remember moving, but the next instant he was kneeling behind her and she was on all fours with her delectable, firm ass in the air. He dipped his finger into her cunt and moaned when she coated the tip with her cream. A snarl left his mouth as he covered her body with his, positioning his dick at her entrance, and he pushed in.

"Oh," Nina moaned.

He paused just in case he was hurting her but figured she was with him every step of the way when she began to rock against him, taking more and more of his hard cock into her tight, wet heat.

His fangs were aching and his gums were itching as if his teeth were trying to lengthen even more, but he didn't think that was possible. Paser nudged her knee with his and she obeyed his silent command by spreading her legs wider. His heart was beating so fast and he was so excited with his need for her that he wasn't sure he could go slowly. He ground his teeth down, not caring that his fangs sank into his lower lip, drawing blood, because it was the only way he seemed to be able to keep himself in check. The urge to slam into her was riding him hard, but this was only her second time making love and he didn't want to hurt her. Ever.

Paser straightened up, grasped her hips in a firm grip to hold her still and began to rock his hips. Ever so slowly he eased his hard cock into her dripping, tight pussy until he was balls-deep. He was shaking so much he felt weak with desire, but his muscles were so full of blood and strength, he felt as if he could take on the world and come out on top.

A moan erupted from his chest when her internal walls clenched around his cock and he swore he felt her cervix open slightly as well.

Paser made a growly noise he'd never heard from himself before and hoped he hadn't scared her. He sounded more like an animal than a man, but he was so horny, needy for her he couldn't seem to help himself.

He eased his cock back until just the tip was still inside her hot cunt and then stroked back in. She whimpered and sighed as if with relief and then groaned when he drew back again.

With each advance and retreat of his dick, he increased the pace of his thrusting until his lower abs were slapping against her ass when their bodies met. Each time he pushed into her, he felt as if he was about to explode. The warm tingles centered in his lower back expanded until his balls were hot and hard with his roiling seed, but there was no way in hell he was going to come before Nina.

He withdrew from her cunt, flipped her over onto her back and dove for her pussy. She gasped and groaned as he licked and sucked every inch of her cunt. The flavor of her cream was the sweetest honey he'd ever had the pleasure to taste and he couldn't get enough.

Paser wrapped one arm around one of her thighs resting his hand on her lower belly as he laved her clit. He loved the little gasps and whimpers she made each time he licked the sensitive little pearl as she creamed for him even more. Reaching up with his free hand, he strummed his thumb over one nipple, pinching and plucking it before moving to the other.

Nina's hips bowed up from the mattress, and while he tried to hold her still, she wouldn't be denied. His tongue slithered down through her folds and he shoved it into her tasty, creamy cunt as far as he could and moaned as her juices covered his tongue and slid down his throat. He sucked and slurped, feeding her desire for him as well as his own.

She hooked one of her legs over his shoulder and he rimmed her pussy before driving his finger in deep. She cried out and shook as she made the slow climb to the peak. Paser added another finger to her tight cunt and pumped them in and out of her sheath. Her internal walls rippled around his digits, and by the way she was panting and mewling, he knew she was getting close.

His dick ached and throbbed and his balls were so hard he wondered if it were possible for them to turn to stone. They were so full and heavy, and yet they had moved up close to his body as if he was about to spurt his load. He tried to push his own hunger to the back of his mind and concentrated on sending Nina over the edge.

He flattened his tongue and swiped it over her clit again and again in sync with his pumping fingers. She was so wet now her juices were dripping from her body in an almost constant stream and he lowered his head every now and then to drink her essence down. He'd never been so in tune with another woman before, but he could feel her inside of him, his body, heart and soul, and he hadn't even claimed her yet. That made him wonder if he'd survive it when he did.

Paser had never felt so much emotion in his life, making it hard for him to fathom which one was the most prominent other than his need to fuck and claim her. He felt like he was on a rollercoaster that had left the rails and had no way of knowing where it would stop or if he'd be alive when it did. He wasn't scared of what he was feeling, though. He wanted to embrace each and every sensation and emotion surging through his heart and body.

He flicked his tongue quickly over her clit and when he felt the heat inside her get hotter, and she writhed as if trying to get away and yet get closer to him, he knew she was right on the cusp. Her cunt walls were so tight now they were nearly strangling his fingers and he couldn't wait to have her wrapped around his hard, aching cock.

And then she seemed to freeze. He glanced up over her body without removing his tongue from her clit or his thrusting fingers from her pussy and moaned at what a beautiful, sexy picture she made. Her neck was arched, her head tilted back and her mouth was open as if on a silent scream.

Just as he rubbed his fingers over her G-spot, she screamed loud enough to wake the dead. He sucked her clit into his mouth, continuing to glide his fingers in and out of her cunt as she came. Her whole body quaked and quivered, her legs trembled and jerked and her pussy convulsed around his digits. Juices gushed from her cunt and he quickly lowered his head and drank her delicious honey. He didn't stop until the spasms began to wane, until only the occasional aftershock wracked her body.

Paser hoped he could keep it together to make her come again before he took his own pleasure, but right now he needed to be buried deep inside of her pussy.

He gave her a last lick, removed his fingers from her sex, and crawled up over her before shoving his hands under her ass and lifting her hips from the bed. The moment the head of his cock brushed against her entrance, he pushed in.

He groaned and sank further and further into her until the tip of his dick was once more touching her womb, before he lowered his body onto hers, braced on his elbows and knees.

Nina wrapped her arms around his neck, her fingers threaded in his hair, and smashed her mouth against his. He loved that she wasn't scared to take what she wanted, what she needed from him, and he gave to her. Their kiss was hot, wild and carnal, and when she wriggled her hips, he knew she was telling him to move. He pulled back and shoved forward, eliciting groans from them both, and as he repeated the action, she wrapped her legs around his waist, which opened her up to him even more.

With each pump of his hips, he drove into her deeper, harder and faster as their bodies pounded together. Although he was worried about hurting her, he couldn't seem to stop. There was a litany in his head that he couldn't ignore and his body seemed to be in sync with that recitation. *Mine. Claim. Mine. Claim.*

The embers which had gone on the backburner sparked to life and each time he stroked his cock into her, they grew hotter and higher.

He released her mouth so they could both gasp for breath, and he stared into her beautiful blue eyes as he made love to her. Even though his body continued to move as he gazed into her eyes, he felt like he was drowning in her and as if they were merging into one being, one body.

The emotional connection they had was phenomenal, but he knew there was more to come. More he needed. More he wanted.

He was so pumped with blood his muscles felt too big for his body, as if they were about to burst from his skin, but he didn't care. All he cared about was making Nina come again before he climaxed and made her his.

When she moaned and her nails dug into the skin at the back of his neck and her pussy grew tighter he knew she was getting close. Each time his pelvis met hers he made sure the light covering of hair on his lower belly and his flesh pressed against her clit. She whimpered and he felt her legs tremble as she clutched him with them. Her pupils dilated even more and the haze over her eyes deepened to a miasma that lightened the blue of her irises.

Her lips parted further and just after she dragged in a deep breath she screamed. Her cunt gripped his cock before releasing him and then she clamped around him again. The fire burning in his spine encompassed his balls and heated his testis so much he wondered if they would burn through his sac. Icy fire raced up his spine and he shouted just before the first spurt of cum erupted from his dick. He didn't remember lowering his head to her neck, the opposite side of where Pen had claimed her, and then he was burying his fangs in the muscle at the crook of her shoulder.

Nina cried out again as she shot back up into another orgasm and his growl of ecstasy joined in. His body shook and shuddered, his cock twitched and pulsed as he spumed into her again and again and again. Paser had never come so hard or long in his life and his vision began to darken, or maybe he'd closed his eyes. He couldn't remember and couldn't see. Just as he thought he was about to pass out from the nirvanic bliss, he felt Nina go limp beneath him. His fangs retracted and he licked the wound, and it took all of his will power and what little strength he had left to lift up so he could see her face.

Her eyes were closed and she was still breathing heavily, but she looked like she'd fallen asleep. Paser looked for the connection he now had with his mate, and elation and love filled his heart to the bursting point. He could feel the tether and followed it back to her. He was so fucking happy moisture filled his eyes and had to blink rapidly so he didn't cry like a baby. He could also feel Pen.

They had been friends for so long he loved him like a brother, but feeling him inside of Nina, their mate only strengthened the bond they already had. He would die for them both if necessary and he knew Pen would do the same for him and their mate.

His heart was whole for the first time in forever and there was a completeness and rightness that he never knew he needed.

Nina didn't stir when he eased his deflating cock from her pussy, nor when he rolled from the bed and stumbled toward the bathroom. He took a couple of minutes to wash up and get some of his equilibrium back, but he wasn't sure that was possible. He'd dreamed of having a woman of his own for so fucking long he couldn't quite believe she was real. It was going to take him a little while to get used to having her at his side. He loved her so much already and it would kill him if anything happened to her, but he was hoping now that she was their mate her body would begin to change like Zara's had.

That gave him pause, because he remembered how worried Set and Sab had been when Zara had gotten sick as her body had adapted to being almost immortal, and the powers and strength that came with being a demigod.

Paser grabbed a washcloth and hurried back to Nina's side. He wasn't surprised to see Pen was lying on his side and gazing at her with awe as if he couldn't quite believe she was real or theirs.

"It's amazing, isn't it?" Pen met his gaze before lowering it back to Nina.

"Yeah." Paser cleared his throat when his voice came out raspy. He hurried to Nina, cleaned her up, and then he climbed into bed with her, tugging the covers up over her cooling, naked body.

"Do you think she's going to be okay?" Paser asked.

Pen frowned and met his gaze again. "You're worried that what happened to Zara will happen to Nina?"

"Yes."

"We can call on Ra if we need to," Pen suggested.

"I know, but sometimes he can't come right away. You know that. And sometimes he doesn't come at all."

"She wouldn't be here if she weren't our mate. She's not going to die, Paser."

"I hope you're right, but I've got a knot in my gut that says otherwise."

"Have a little faith. Isn't that what Ra always says? Things happen for a reason. We might not always understand it or agree with it, but you know the sun god wouldn't let us find our mate only to take her away from us again."

"I hope you're right, Pen."

Pen grinned. "I usually am."

"You're such a dick sometimes."

"You like it when I'm being a dick. Admit it, if it wasn't for me, you would never laugh."

"You're full of shit." Paser smirked. "You're the one who's always frowning."

"And you don't?" Pen quirked his eyebrow.

"Never."

"Liar."

Paser felt a little better after their ridiculous banter and settled down next to Nina before pulling her into his arms. Pen moved up close to her back and wrapped an arm around her waist.

He would give her a few hours of sleep and then he was going to wake her just to make sure she was all right. He wouldn't be able to sleep or stop worrying if he didn't take care of his mate.

Chapter Nine

Nina felt as if she was floating in a sea of mist. Everywhere she looked, there were wispy swirls of gray, and yet she knew she wasn't really conscious. She could feel Pen and Paser at her sides, cuddling close to her, and even though she tried to surface, she couldn't. She had no idea what was happening to her and she was scared.

She could feel surges of power thrumming through her blood, yet every time she tried to move, she couldn't. What concerned her even more, though, was the fact she was burning for her mates, again, yet she knew it hadn't been that long since they'd made love to her and claimed her.

She felt fine. No, that wasn't quite true, but she wasn't sick. She felt energized and her skin was so sensitive it felt as if it was crawling. The low hum of energy was getting stronger and stronger, and so was the desire to have both her mates make to love to her again and again. Her body seemed to be changing and she wasn't sure she liked what she was feeling. For a moment or two, she wondered if she was caught in another dream where the shadow demons and their master were waiting to pounce, but she didn't feel any evil nearby. Plus, there wasn't any of the black oiliness she'd felt before.

Nina felt as if she was caught between two planes of existence where she was awake enough to know what was going on about her, but too tired and heavy to wake. It was the weirdest sensation she'd ever felt.

She sighed when Pen kissed her shoulder, and again when Paser rubbed his cheek on the top of her head. It was a little disconcerting to feel them inside of her heart, two little sparks which had filled the empty spaces in her soul. She'd never felt so loved, content and complete in her life, and she wanted to be with them, so why couldn't she make herself wake up?

Another wave of heat surged through her body and centered in her cunt, causing the inner walls to clench and cream to weep out. Now that she'd had a taste of her mates' lovemaking, it was as if she were addicted and wouldn't be able to stop until they took her, until she hit that high, like a drug addict looking for the next hit.

The heat grew and seeped from her pussy up into her womb and belly. Her legs twitched, her areolae contracted and her nipples hardened. She tried to roll over, but her body was so heavy it wouldn't obey.

She groaned when Pen caressed down her body from just beneath her breast to her stomach, over her hip and upper thigh, before making the return journey. Paser threaded his fingers with hers and that was the moment she was able to open her eyes. The moment she did, she knew she was different. The colors in the room were so vibrant they nearly hurt to look at. The ceiling was so white it almost blinded her. Each caress over her skin felt like a deep-tissue massage she'd once had, and while she hadn't like that sensation, she loved the way her mates' hands felt on her skin.

"How are you feeling, baby?" Pen asked.

"I don't know." She didn't want to alarm them but she couldn't lie. She felt really strange and was beginning to get really scared.

"What's wrong, sweetheart?" Paser cupped her face and frowned as he gazed into her eyes.

"I-I don't know if I can explain it."

Pen sat up against the headboard and lifted her up next to him. Paser shifted until he was right next to her in the same position.

"When I was asleep, I wasn't really. I could hear and feel everything, but my body was so heavy I couldn't control it."

"Shit, that doesn't sound good." Pen frowned.

"Yeah, I was kinda scared. My body feels hypersensitive. The thing that worried me the most was that I also feel really energized, as if I could run for miles and not get tired."

"Your body's changing," Paser explained. "We told you it would, sweetheart. I don't think you have anything to be scared about. We'll be with you every step of the way."

"Okay." Nina sighed with relief. "Thank you. That was one of my concerns."

"What are the others?" Pen shifted so that he didn't have to turn his head so far.

"I'm really hot and itchy."

"Let me feel." Paser placed his hand on her forehead. "You haven't got a fever."

"The heat is on the inside and it feels like it's trying to devour me." Although she tried not to cry, tears welled up and spilled down her cheeks.

Pen placed his hand on her belly, the tips of his fingers brushing against the top of her bare mound, and she cried out. Not because she was in pain, but because all of a sudden she was so horny she felt like she was going to explode.

"It's the bond." Pen said.

"What's happening to me?" Nina sobbed and covered her mouth, trying to stifle the noise of her gasping breaths.

"Do you trust us, sweetheart?"

"You know I do," she wailed before clutching at her stomach. "Make it stop."

"We will," Pen said as he lifted her into his arms.

She ended up straddling his waist and grasping tightly to his shoulders, her nails digging into his skin.

Before she could take her next breath he was lowering her onto his hard cock. A long, low moan emitted from her mouth and she sighed as a semblance of relief eased the heat in her body.

"We are going to love you together, Nina. We need to do this so that the bond between us strengthens. The only way I can explain what's happening is that you're in some kind of mating heat."

"What?"

"Shh, sweetheart," Paser whispered against her ear as he moved up close to her back. "Everything will be fine."

Nina nodded, not sure if she believed them, because she didn't feel fine. She felt so horny she wanted to claw the skin from her body to make it stop itching. The heat was building again and she wasn't sure she could take much more.

Pen cupped the back of her neck and pulled her mouth down to his. She opened to him and sighed with pleasure as his tongue stroked into her mouth, swirling and twirling with and around hers. His hands caressed from her waist to her hip and he gripped her pelvis firmly in his big, manly hands as he spread his legs wider and pulling her tighter against his chest. She didn't care that her ass was probably in Paser's face. All she cared about was her mates taking the deep, burning ache inside of her away.

Nina tried to lift up but Pen wouldn't allow it, nor did he let her stop the kiss. She knew why a moment later. Paser kissed her shoulder, and when he caressed a cool, moist finger over her anus, she jolted.

Pen finally broke the kiss before nibbling on her earlobe.

"Just relax, sweetheart," Paser crooned as he continued to massage her rosette. "We're going to make you feel so good."

She shivered and moaned when the tip of his finger penetrated her back entrance, and was surprised by how good it felt. She'd never even thought about anal sex before, nor had she suspected she would like having her ass touched, but she did. Her walls contracted, making her and Pen groan as cream leaked from her cunt.

"She likes what you're doing to her," Pen said in a raspy voice. "She just covered me with her cum. I can fill it dripping onto my balls."

"Oh god."

"Easy, baby." Pen licked the tendon up her neck before scraping his teeth over her skin and sucking it into his mouth.

The heat was almost interminable now and goose bumps erupted over her entire body in reaction. She whimpered when Paser added another finger to ass and sobbed with pleasure when he began to stroke them in and out of her anus, while scissoring them to stretch her muscles.

"I can't take it," she cried and tried to shove back onto Paser's fingers to take him deeper inside of her.

"Yes you can, Nina. You can take it. You can take my cock in your ass. Can't you, sweetheart?"

"Yes." She gasped and strained toward the release she was hovering on the edge of, but for some reason, she couldn't go over. She whimpered with frustration and then moaned with disappointment when Paser drew his finger out of her star. She'd been so close, but now that she no longer had her ass filled by him, she felt empty.

"Take a nice, deep breath and hold it for me, sweetheart. When I push in, breathe out, push back and try to relax."

Nina nodded to let him know she'd heard him, but she was so intent on having both her mates inside of her body, making love to her, she couldn't think of any words to say.

She inhaled deeply when she felt the head of Paser's lubed cock against her pucker and held her breath. The skin around her ass burned slightly as the tip of his dick pressed in, but it wasn't a horrible pain. In fact, it just seemed to make the hunger burning inside of her more intense.

Nina released the air in her lungs, and as she did, the tautness in her muscles dissipated slightly. As she drew in another breath, she pushed back against Paser's cock.

"Shit!" Paser groaned. "Her ass is so fucking hot and tight."

"Hurry up!" Pen gasped. "I'm not going to last much longer."

"I don't want to hurt her."

"You won't." Nina exhaled before inhaling again, and when Paser stroked deeper into her ass, she pressed back until she felt his body up against hers.

"Don't do that again, Nina. I could have hurt you."

"Move!" Nina demanded.

"Let's give our mate what she wants." Pen nodded to Paser and then they both began to move.

Paser withdrew from her anus and as he stroked back in, Pen eased from her cunt. Nina was shaking so much she couldn't move her body the way she wanted to, so she held onto Pen instead. Her body was going up in flames and each time they drove into her, the fire grew hotter, the flames grew bigger. They counter-thrust one after the other. In. Out. In. Out.

The friction of having two cocks in her body, gliding along her internal walls, was so good that she couldn't have described it if she wanted to. The tension built higher and higher, causing her to shake and shiver, moan and groan. Their bodies slapped together in a loud cacophony of carnal delight and she raced toward the cliff edge.

Paser drove his cock deep into her ass and then Pen shoved up into her cunt. She didn't know how she was remaining upright because her legs were shaking almost spasmodically now.

The molten liquid that was racing through her veins was so hot she wondered if her blood would boil and dry right up, but she couldn't fall over the edge. She sobbed with frustration and hunger, and just as she was about to demand they do something, Pen pushed her up from his chest until she almost sitting upright and he followed. His mouth latched onto one of her nipples and he sucked it hard into his mouth. Paser's hand glided over her belly to the top of her pussy and the tip of his finger pressed on her clit.

Nina screamed. The fire consumed her. White and blue flashed before her eyes as she went up in smoke. Her whole body jerked and juddered as her internal walls clenched and released in convulsive, reflexive contractions as she orgasmed. She was only vaguely aware of Paser shoving into her ass before holding still. His shout of completion was almost drowned out by the loud roaring in her ears. A couple of strokes later, Pen's yell joined Paser's voice as he, too, climaxed. Each time their cocks pulsed, her cunt clenched in answer as her orgasm went on and on.

The heat intensified into an inferno when both of her mates sank their fangs into the crook of her shoulders and neck. The flashes of light faded until all she saw was black, and as she gasped for air, her body slumped down onto Pen's chest. Her awareness of her mates and her surroundings faded until she passed out.

* * * *

"Geezus," Pen panted, trying to regain his breath. He felt like he had been fighting for days he was so weak.

"That was…" Paser groaned as he eased his deflating cock from Nina's ass. He caressed her butt cheeks and flopped down onto the bed. "Is she all right?"

"I don't know. She passed out." Pen frowned with concern. He wrapped his arms around her and rolled them both onto their sides.

"She's not even breathing heavy anymore." Paser lifted up onto an elbow.

Pen's cock slipped from Nina's body as he shifted down the bed. He placed his ear to her chest and sighed with relief when he heard her lungs fill with air and felt the movement beneath his cheek. That's when he felt the heat building inside her.

"Go fill the tub with cool water," Pen ordered as he sat up and placed his hand on her forehead. The longer he left his hand against the skin, the hotter she became.

Paser stood and walked toward the bathroom.

"Hurry Paser. She's sick." Pen scooped Nina up into his arms and he watched her closely as he walked. She seemed to be out cold, totally oblivious to anything around her. His heart flipped, missing a beat as fear for his mate assailed him, and as he tried to find the bond he and Paser had just formed with her, he couldn't.

Paser looked up as Pen carried her toward the bath, reached out a hand to place on her forehead and frowned. "Shit!"

"We need to cool her body down. Her skin's getting way too hot."

Paser nodded. "What do you want me to do?"

"I don't know." Pen stepped into the filling tub, trying to ignore the way the cold water lapped at his calves and the goose bumps racing over his skin. His comfort was unimportant right now. They needed to take care of their mate. He drew in a deep breath and sat in the deep spa bath. He didn't exhale until he'd bitten back his gasp at having to sit in the cold water. "Get a cloth. You can wash her while I hold her."

Paser grabbed a cloth from the cupboard under the vanity and, after dipping in the water, began to caress it over Nina's body.

Pen was becoming really worried now. Still, she hadn't twitched or moved a single muscle. In his long years of living, a feverish person always reacted to being sunk into cold water. Whether it was a moan, or they started shivering or thrashing, he'd always seen a reaction. There was no such sign from Nina.

"I can't feel her through the bond," Pen whispered as fear permeated his heart. He'd been able to feel more emotion from her before they had mated with her, and that had intensified after claiming her the first time, but now there was nothing.

"I can't either," Paser said in a tight voice. "Should I go and get Zara, Set and Sab?"

"What can they do?"

"I don't know," Paser snapped, "but I'll be damned if I won't do nothing."

"You are doing something, Paser. You're washing her and helping to cool her down."

"It's not enough."

"What else is there to do?"

"Fucked if I know," Paser roared his answer.

Pen looked down at Nina. Again, she hadn't moved. It was like she was in a coma. He wondered if she could hear them but couldn't move or respond. "We need to talk to her."

"What's that going to do?" Paser asked.

"Hell if I know, but I've heard that if you talk to someone who is locked in a coma, they can hear you. Maybe the sound of our voices will bring her back."

"You think she's in a coma?" Paser almost whispered the question and Pen could hear and feel the fear he had for their mate. He was just as scared and worried, but they needed to keep it together for Nina.

"I don't know, Paser, but it's worth a try."

Paser nodded before dipping the cloth into the cold water again, and then he dripped it over her hair. "It's not enough. We need to totally submerge her but keep her face out of the water. A human loses a lot of heat through their head. Maybe by having her head in the water, it will cool her faster."

Pen shifted to his hands and knees, supporting Nina's body so that she didn't fall under the surface. He placed one hand beneath the back of her neck and the other under her lower back, and carefully eased her deeper into the tub. He nearly sighed with relief when he saw goose bumps emerge over her skin, but he was still concerned about her lack of reaction. "Do you think it's working?"

"I don't know." Pen leaned over the edge of the bath and placed his hand on her forehead. "She still feels too hot to me."

"How long are we supposed to keep her in here? She could end up getting sick." Pen glanced at Paser.

"She shouldn't be sick now." Paser's voice held a hint of frustration. "We mated her. She should never be sick again."

"I know…" Pen's breath caught in his throat when Nina moaned. He tried to feel her through their bond, but there was still nothing.

However, he began to hope that she was coming out of whatever held her in its grip. That was until she started convulsing.

"Fuck! Get her out quick." Paser reached over to help Pen lift her from the bath. They wrapped her in a towel and placed her on her side on the bed. Her body was rigid and jerking uncontrollably, and there was nothing he or Paser could do except make sure she didn't choke on her own vomit if she got sick, or bit her own tongue.

Pen tried to pry her jaw open, but it was clamped so tight and he didn't want to hurt her by forcing it apart.

"Get something we can put in her mouth. I don't want her swallowing her own tongue."

Paser raced from the room and came back with a wooden spoon of all things, but the handle was thick and hopefully Nina wouldn't be able to bite through it or break it. The last thing they needed was for her to end up cut or with splinters. Pen carefully pried her lips and teeth apart before Paser slipped the handle over her tongue and between her teeth.

It seemed to take forever for her muscles to stop spasming and for the tautness to leave, but finally, her body went lax. He and Paser both had their hands on her so she hadn't been able to move too far as she'd fitted. They both still had their hands on her and Pen thought that the heat was starting to leave her body.

"Does she feel cooler to you?" Paser asked.

Pen sighed with relief, glad that Paser thought her fever was diminishing, too. "Yes."

"Thank the gods."

Pen agreed, but he wouldn't stop worrying until he was looking into her gorgeous blue eyes. He'd never been so fucking scared in his life and hoped to never be again. His mate sick and in pain was too much for him to bear. He'd rather it had been him with the fever and convulsing than watching Nina go through something like that. His heart and soul couldn't take seeing her so ill.

Chapter Ten

Nina felt sick to her stomach, and she was encased in a heat so intense she thought maybe she'd died and was stuck in hell. She had no idea where she was or who was with her, and she was scared out of her mind. She could hear voices, but none of their words made sense, and no matter how hard she tried to remember where she'd been before she started feeling ill, she couldn't.

And then her feverish body was submerged into what felt like ice, and while she wanted to scream and cry, she couldn't move or talk. She was trapped inside of her own body, and though she struggled to surface, she couldn't find the light, the way out. She had no idea if she were awake or dreaming, but when she tried to see, all she saw was a deep, dark blackness.

A twinge of memory flitted across her mind as if she been here before, but she couldn't seem to hold onto the thought. She concentrated on trying to move her body, but it wouldn't obey her brain's command, not even her little finger. Even though she was cold, she was also hot, too hot, and she was worried. Worried that she was either dying or already dead.

The fire began to build again and the cold around her began to heat, adding to the flames licking at her insides. She felt as if she were moving but didn't think that was the case, since she had no control over herself at all. All of a sudden, her body went rigid and then began to jerk spasmodically. Her teeth ground together, the grating sound loud and irritating to her own ears.

Firm fingers dug into the joint of her jaw and her teeth were pried apart. Her stomach roiled and she wanted to swallow, but she couldn't even manage to do that. Drool trickled from her mouth and onto her face, and she knew she should be embarrassed, but she was too sick to care. After what seemed like hours, the heat burning her insides began to wane and her tense, jerking muscles started to relax. She couldn't believe how tired she was, exhausted to the point of being stupefied, and with a sigh of relief she sank deeper into the darkness and slept.

* * * *

Nina had no idea how long she'd been asleep, but the moment she returned to consciousness, she smiled. She forced her eyelids open and blinked a few times to clear her blurry vision, and smiled again when she felt and saw Pen and Paser asleep beside her. They were so damn handsome and they were all hers.

When she perused each of their faces, she frowned. They both had dark circles beneath their eyes as if they'd lost out on a lot of sleep. She didn't know why that would be, because they just made love to and mated her.

Shouldn't they feel as happy and relaxed as she did?

Something was wrong. She felt the certainty deep in her gut, and even though she wanted to wake them and ask them, she didn't. They looked so tired and she figured they needed to rest longer. Maybe making love to and mating her had taken a lot of their energy.

Nina would talk to them when they woke up. When she moved, she frowned at the dull ache in her muscles but put it down to the sex they'd had. She'd been a virgin, after all, and wasn't used to using her muscles like that. She gave a mental shrug, carefully moved to her hands and knees and crawled down the bed, trying not to disturb her men. When her feet touched the floor, she gave them a last, lingering look and hurried toward the bathroom. She needed the facilities in a bad way. Her bladder was aching since it was so full.

After she'd relieved herself, she showered, dressed, brushed her teeth and headed out of the apartment. She hadn't had time to explore her men's home and the urge to do so wouldn't be ignored.

She stepped out into the hall and listened, but couldn't hear any voices coming from the kitchen dining area and figured everyone else must still be asleep or ensconced in their own apartments. As she walked down the hall, the ache in her muscles lessened. The more she moved, the more in tune to her body she became. She felt energized and stronger than she'd ever felt in her life. A bubble of laughter formed, but she quickly swallowed it down because she didn't want to make too much noise and wake the others if they were still sleeping.

When she got to a wide door in the hallway, she peeked into the room and gasped. It was the most amazing room she'd ever seen. The walls were covered in color paintings that looked like they were Egyptian, and when she walked further into the room and looked up, she could see the stars twinkling in the dark sky. The ceiling wasn't actually a ceiling. The center was shaped like a pyramid and it was all glass, and the glass tip had a thin layer of water over it, but was deeper over the descending slopes of the three-dimensional, triangular shape. It was absolutely spectacular.

Nina wondered how the hell they'd built this place, and underwater, no less. There was still so much she didn't know and added the how of it to her list of things to ask. As she moved about the room, studying the hieroglyphs depicted on the walls, she realized how relaxed she felt. Peace and tranquility washed over her in gentle waves and she sighed with contentment.

She moved back to the middle of the room and looked up toward the sky. As she stood there, staring into space, she felt a surge of power wash over and through her. She spun around and looked to every corner of the room but couldn't see anything, and then she felt a tingling heat on her skin right above her left breast and over her left and right shoulder blades. Her skin tingled, and her body hummed with peace, love, and happiness, and even as she tried to contain it, she couldn't. She laughed out loud and spun in a circle with her arms out to her sides.

Nina had never felt so free and happy, but she loved the feeling and put it down to having two mates. It was then she remembered the connection she was supposed to have with Pen and Paser, and looked into her heart to see if she could find it, feel it.

The moment she turned inward, she saw the glowing strings embedded in her heart and soul, and followed them back to her men. She gasped when she felt fear and worry coming from them, and as she spun toward the door, something clicked into place. The emotions intensified and nearly brought her to her knees.

She ran toward their apartment, her men, her heart beating hard in her chest, and she blinked when she stood before the door to their apartment. She shouldn't be back at that door so soon. The underground base was way bigger than she'd ever imagined. It had taken her at least ten minutes to stroll along the corridor and the spectacular room she'd found.

If she hadn't been so worried about her men, she would have timed herself as she ran back down the hall, but right now she needed to see that her mates were all right. Nina opened and closed the door quietly, and when she entered the bedroom, she sighed with relief. Pen and Paser appeared to be fine and were both still sound asleep.

She frowned when she remembered that they'd told her the sentinels hunted the shadow demons at night and wondered why they weren't out searching for the demonic.

Nina figured the others must be out searching for the shadow demons trying to keep humanity safe, but surely Set and Sab wouldn't have taken Zara along with them.

Although she would love to fight alongside her guys, she didn't think they would let her tag along. She'd probably be more of a hindrance than a help. That was unless Zara had been trained to fight the shadow demons, too, but if the other woman had only just been made immortal, surely she wouldn't have all the skills necessary to fight off the demonic so soon.

Nina decided then and there that she would convince them to train her. There was no way she was going to let them out night after night while she sat home worrying until they walked back in the door. She'd never been someone to sit back and wait, and she wouldn't be now.

Nina glanced at the clock on the bedside table and gasped when she saw it was only four in the morning. She was so full of energy she could barely stand still. Pen blinked and when his eyes landed on her, he jumped out of bed and was pulling her into his arms before she had time to blink or draw another breath.

"Nina, are you okay? How do you feel? Do you need me to get you anything? What are you doing out of bed? You should still be resting."

"Whoa. Slow down."

"Nina!" Paser yelled, and then he was at her back. "You have no idea how happy I am to see you up and about. How are you feeling, sweetheart? Do you feel sick? Feverish?"

Nina could feel and hear the worry radiating off of them and wondered what the hell was going on. She moved from between them toward the bed, sat on the edge and smiled wryly when her empty belly protested loudly.

"I'm fine."

"Thank the gods," Pen whispered as he knelt at her feet and pressed his cheek to her belly.

"We've been so worried about you, sweetheart." Paser sat beside her, slung an arm around her shoulders and pulled her up tight against his body.

"I can feel what you are feeling. In fact, I felt fear just before you both woke up. Why were you scared?"

Pen lifted his head and looked deeply into her eyes. "You don't remember?"

"Remember what?"

"You were sick, Nina."

"What?"

"We thought you were going to die," Paser said. Nina heard the anguish in his voice and felt the lingering emotion of both of their fear.

"How did I get sick? All I remember is feeling very, very horny and you both making love to me."

Pen and Paser took turns explaining that she had been out for three days and nights. She could hear the anxiety in their voices and the distress they'd endured over her.

Tears burned her eyes. "I'm sorry. I didn't mean to put you through that."

"Don't apologize, baby. We should be the ones apologizing to you. We are the reason you got sick in the first place." Pen ran his fingers through his hair.

"How do you figure that?"

"Your body has gone through the transformation because we mated you," Paser answered quietly, his chin dipping toward his chest as he lowered his gaze.

"Did you know I would get sick?"

"Not really," Pen replied.

"What do you mean by that?"

"Zara went through something similar, but Set and Sab called on Ra to heal her. They couldn't handle watching their mate go through such torture."

"It can't have been that bad." Nina smiled. "I don't remember it and I feel fantastic. Please don't blame yourselves. I agreed, wanted to be your mate. Even if I'd known I'd get sick, I wouldn't have changed my mind."

"Are you sure?" Paser asked.

"Yes. Don't dwell on what was. It's in the past."

Paser cupped her face and met her gaze. "I love you, Nina Page."

Nina swallowed around the lump of emotion constricting her throat and tried to blink the tears back. "I love you, too, Paser Ebo."

Paser leaned down and kissed her passionately. His tongue twirled around and glided along hers. By the time he lifted his head, they were both breathless.

Pen stood, clasped her hand and tugged her to her feet. "I love you, baby."

The tears of happiness wouldn't be denied anymore. She smiled tremulously as she looked at her mate through the moisture. She had to take a couple of deep breaths before she could speak. "I love you, too, Pentu Chatha."

"I know you do, baby. I can feel your love." Pen smiled, and all the concern and fear he'd harbored in his heart washed away.

"I can feel you, too." Nina turned and held her free hand out toward Paser. He surged to his feet and threaded his fingers through hers. "I can feel both of you."

"We are going to spend a lot of time loving you, sweetheart."

"Good. I can't wait." Nina smiled and kissed both her men lightly on the lips. "How did you guys get the glass pyramid roof under water? How did you get this…base under a lake?"

"We didn't." Paser grinned.

"Then who did?" She frowned with confusion.

"Ra did."

"Are you kidding me?" Nina asked, but she could tell by their expressions they weren't. "Did he use his godly powers or something?"

"I would presume so, but we weren't here when he built it."

"Where were you?"

"We have no idea," Pen answered.

"What?"

"We had just been transformed into sentinels, sweetheart. Apparently we slept for three long days." Paser tugged her into his arms and held her tight against his chest. Pen moved up and pressed his front against her back.

"Ha, that sounds familiar."

"Shit!" Pen frowned. "I'd forgotten all about that."

"Well, I suppose that's to be expected since you're all so old. Senility might be setting in." Nina giggled and then burst out laughing at the incredulous expressions on her mates' faces.

Pen and Paser started chuckling and they full-out laughed. The sound of their deep basses sent shivers of need surging to her core, but she pushed her lust aside. She was so happy and in love.

Right then, she was floating on a high. She felt almost euphoric with joy and love.

God, it was great to be alive.

"We need to pull some clothes on," Paser said after he'd regained his breath and moved toward the chair where his and Pen's clothes had been draped.

Nina sighed with disappointment as they both dressed. She loved seeing their muscular chests, shoulders, arms and legs. They only had boxers on when they got out of bed, and as much as she wanted to ask them to strip again so they could make love, she was too hungry for food.

Her stomach was still growling up a storm, begging for nourishment.

"Come on, baby." Pen held his hand out to her. "We need to get you something to eat."

"Okay." Nina clasped his hand and let him lead her out to the kitchen. She decided to broach the subject of going out with them each night while they ate.

Chapter Eleven

Paser sat back in his chair, contented to watch Nina. She'd devoured the roast beef sandwiches he'd made as well as the fruit he'd cut up.

"Are the others out hunting?" Nina asked after taking a sip of her tea.

"I wouldn't call it hunting, but yes," Pen answered.

"Including Zara," Nina asked.

Paser had an idea where Nina was heading and hid his smile. He could feel her excitement through their bond.

"Yes." Pen narrowed his eyes at Nina, but Paser knew it wasn't because he was angry. His friend was trying not to laugh at their mate's roundabout way to get what she wanted. To hunt with them.

"Did Set and Sab train her?"

"Yes," Paser answered calmly. Inside, he was roaring with laughter. Their mate was sneaky when she wanted to get her own way. He loved her so much and would do anything to make her happy, even train her to become a sentinel if that was what she wanted.

"So?"

"So what?" Pen asked.

Nina rolled her eyes. "Come on, guys, you know what. I can feel you laughing through the bond."

"You can?" Paser asked, awed that she was so in tune to them already. He didn't think Zara had been able to pick up on Set's and Sab's emotions as quickly as Nina was able to pick up theirs.

"Of course I can. Just as you already know I want you to train me." Nina leaned back in her chair with a sigh, picked up her mug of tea and took a sip.

"Is that really what you want, baby?" Pen covered her hand and squeezed. "Don't think you have to do this if you don't want to."

"How can you ask me that? I need to know how to fight these…things. I have never been so scared in my life as when you met me that night and when I was caught up in that nightmare. I felt so helpless and I don't want to feel like that again. I need to know how to take them down."

"We'll keep you safe, sweetheart." Paser leaned over and kissed her temple. He would give his last breath so that Nina could live.

"I know you will, but you can't follow me into a dream. Can you?"

Pen shook his head. "Not that we know."

"So it only makes sense that I'm prepared and know how to fight. You can't invade my dreams and can't be with me every minute of every day."

"She's right." Paser sighed. He hated the thought of Nina fighting the demonic, but he and Pen couldn't follow her into her dreams. At least he didn't think they could. He would feel a lot better if she knew how to protect herself in case there was ever a need. Of course, if the worst happened and she could defend herself, they would be able to get to her on time. He hoped.

"Okay," Pen agreed after a few moments. "When do you want to start training?"

"No time like the present."

Paser met Pen's gaze and nodded. They quickly cleaned up the dishes and headed to the large gym.

"Wow." Nina's awed whisper as they entered the gym room made him smile. She looked like a kid in a candy store.

"Are those swords?" She pointed to the sickle-shaped swords hanging on the wall.

"Yes," Paser replied.

"Are they glowing?" Nina squinted her eyes as she stared at the golden blades.

"Yes." Pen walked across the room and plucked a sword from the wall before turning around to hand it to Nina.

"Why does the blade glow?"

"We think it's because of Ra." Paser moved up behind Nina as she took the proffered sword from Pen.

"It's not as heavy as I thought it would be." Nina lifted the sword up and down.

"Hold it like this." Paser adjusted her grip and, when Pen moved back, moved her arm in arcs so she could get a feel for the weapon. "Always have the curved part of the blade facing away from you. If you have it toward you, the tip could snag on something and get stuck."

"I'll remember." Nina moved about when Paser stepped back. She looked so sexy swinging the blade from side to side.

"Okay. We'll come back to the sword at a later date." Pen took the sword and hung it back on the wall. "We need to test your speed and endurance. Sometimes you'll have to move fast so that the demonic or the possessed humans can't get a hold on you."

"What do you want me to do?"

"Go for a run on the treadmill." Paser led her over to the machine, showed her how it worked, and then walked over to the weights. He and Pen added weight plates to the bars and began to lift. When Paser glanced at Pen, he saw his friend staring at Nina as she warmed up with a walk. Neither of them could keep their eyes off of their mate.

"Do you think the shadow demons will try to get to her again?" Paser asked, and he turned to stare at Nina again. She was jogging now and he couldn't help but smile when he saw that she was grinning. She hit the button on the treadmill and then laughed as the machine sped up until she was sprinting. She was beautiful. Even though she wasn't very tall, her legs seemed to go on forever. They were long, lithe and toned. Her ass was a nice handful, but was firm as well as being soft and plump. She was more than he could have ever imagined a beautiful and sexy woman to be and she was all theirs.

"I don't know. I hope not," Pen murmured.

Paser looked over at him and tried to remember what he'd asked. He sucked in a ragged breath when his words came back to him. A knot of dread formed in his gut and he tried to dispel it, but no matter how hard he tried, it wouldn't be dislodged. He just hoped that it wasn't a sign of things to come.

* * * *

As Nina sprinted on the treadmill, she felt invigorated. She'd never been much of a runner. Of course, she'd practically walked everywhere since she didn't have a car and couldn't afford one. She was surprised to find how fast she could move, but what astounded her was the fact she wasn't huffing and puffing.

"Slow it down, now, sweetheart."

She met Paser's gaze, but looked beyond him when she saw movement toward the back wall. She stumbled when she saw Pen lifting weights. The bar was packed full of metal plates, and although his biceps were bulging and rippling, he didn't look like he was having any trouble holding the huge burden.

"Whoa." Paser snagged her around the waist with one arm and lifted her off the treadmill and against his chest. "Are you okay?"

"Yes." Nina cleared her throat as she met his gaze and gave him a chagrinned smile. "I got distracted."

"You can't afford to let anything to distract you in a fight, sweetheart. You could end up getting seriously hurt or killed."

"Aren't I immortal now?"

"Yes, and we heal quickly, but we can still be killed."

"How?"

"Decapitation."

Nina covered her mouth with her hand. Just the thought of her mates losing their heads made her feel sick to her stomach and pain pierce her heart. The moment her hand touched her mouth, she gasped. She pulled her hand away and stared at the bead of blood on her palm near the base of her thumb. She looked up at Paser and lifted her hand to her mouth again. This time she used her fingers instead of her whole hand to explore her mouth.

Fear shot through her when she felt the tips of sharp teeth. "What…"

"Don't panic, Nina." Paser pulled her tighter against his chest, hugging her with both of his arms.

"Do I have fangs?"

"Yes."

"Why?" She wailed her question and pushed against his shoulders. "Let me down."

"What's wrong?" Pen asked as he came to stand next to Nina.

"Nina just discovered her fangs."

"Oh."

Nina turned her glare to Pen. "Oh. Is that all you can say? Why didn't you tell me I would get fangs?"

"I thought Zara told you," Paser frowned.

"She did."

"Then why are you so surprised? Why are you scared?" Pen asked.

"I didn't believe her," Nina whispered.

"Come here, baby." Pen grasped her wrist and tugged her toward him.

He wrapped her in his arms and rubbed his cheek on the top of her head. The tension in her muscles dissipated and she sighed as she leaned against his chest. Paser pressed his chest to her back. She felt so safe and protected between her two mates and never wanted to leave. The hunger to make love to them again surged into her pussy, making her wet, but what she needed more right now was answers. She felt as if her life was out of her control and that scared her a little.

Nina didn't regret mating with Paser and Pen. In fact, the opposite was true. She'd found love. How could she deny them when they were already so firmly entrenched into her heart and soul? What she was having trouble with was how she felt as if she were floundering along with no direction because she still had so few answers.

"What's wrong, sweetheart?" Paser rubbed his hands up and down her arms in an offer of comfort.

"I just feel like I'm drifting with no direction."

"Why?" Pen drew back and frowned at her.

"Because I don't know enough. My whole life has changed in the blink of an eye."

Nina sighed when she felt a surge of pain in her heart and immediately felt contrite, because the pain wasn't hers. She moved out from between her mates so she could see their faces and frowned when she saw the blank expressions they'd assumed.

"Please, don't be mad at me."

"We're not angry," Pen said.

She reached out and clasped their hands, threading their fingers together, and hoped she hadn't hurt them so badly they wouldn't forgive her. "I'm sorry. I didn't mean to hurt you. I don't regret my decision to mate with you. I love you both, so much."

"Does that scare you?" Paser squeezed her hand.

"Sometimes. My world has been turned upside-down in a few short days. It's a lot to digest." Nina drew in a ragged breath. "Don't think I don't love you or blame either of you. I'm so happy you came along when you did, because if you hadn't, I would probably be dead and wouldn't have never met either of you. I feel as if I'm going a little insane. There's so much I have to learn and I'm not sure I'll ever be enough."

"Stop!" Paser snapped. "Get those thoughts out of your head right now. You're everything to us."

"Baby, you are the most important person in our lives. How can you think you would never be enough?" Pen asked in a hoarse voice.

"I want to fight by your side. I want to be able to protect you if necessary, but I'm not sure I'll ever be as strong as you are. I've never had to battle anyone and the thought of not being able to do so scares the hell out of me."

"Nina." Paser cupped her face in his hand. "You are perfect."

"No I'm not."

"Let me finish," Paser commanded. "I didn't mean that we have you up on a pedestal. We know you're not perfect and god knows we're not, either. You're perfect for us. You have so much love in your heart, and we are honored and humble that you've come to love us. The other stuff is inconsequential. You'll learn just like we did. You don't think we knew what we were doing overnight, do you? It took us years to become proficient with swords and fighting. We were slaves before Ra found us and turned us. The only fighting we'd ever done was the fight for survival."

"Paser's right." Pen released her hand and tugged her against him. "Rome wasn't built in a day, sweetheart."

Nina sighed as she rubbed her cheek on his chest and inhaled his delectable scent. Paser moved in behind her again and she felt so warm, safe and protected between her mates.

"You're a lot stronger than you think." Pen kissed the top of her head. "And from the way you handled that sword earlier, I'd say you're a natural."

"Do you think so?"

"We know so." Paser squeezed her waist. "You handle a sword better than I did when we first started on this adventure."

"Thank you." Nina closed her eyes and listened to the soothing thump of Pen's heartbeat. "Will I have to drink blood now?"

"Ah." Paser turned her around and lifted her into his arms.

Nina clutched at his shoulders and wrapped her legs around his waist for balance. "What?"

"That's the crux of your worries right now, isn't it?" Paser asked.

"Yes."

"Why didn't you just come out and ask, baby?" Pen questioned.

Nina buried her face in Paser's neck. "I didn't want to offend you."

"Look at me, Nina," Paser demanded.

She lifted her head and met his gaze. "Nothing you say or do will ever offend us. We're your mates and we are yours. If something is on your mind, then talk to us, damn it. We can't help you if we don't know what the problem is."

Nina nodded.

"What did Zara tell you about drinking blood?" Pen ran a hand down her back and then squeezed her ass cheek.

Nina's arousal had gone back to a low simmer, but flared up again.

"She said that I wouldn't need to drink blood, but I might need to if I get injured."

"She was right." Paser said. "We only ever consume blood if we lose too much. We aren't vampires, sweetheart."

"Okay. Sorry for all the drama." Nina's taut muscles relaxed now that her mates had affirmed she wouldn't need to survive on blood. The thought of doing so made her feel ill.

"You have no need to apologize, baby."

Paser released her when she wiggled to get down.

"Promise me something." Pen snagged her waist so she couldn't walk away.

"What?"

"If something is bothering you, come talk to us. Please?"

Nina nodded and smiled. "I will."

"Good." Pen slanted his mouth over hers and kissed her passionately. Nina kissed him back just as hungrily, and if she hadn't heard voices, she would have started tugging at his clothes. She was horny and needed her mates, but it looked like she was going to have to take a raincheck.

Pen released her lips and Paser immediately stepped in to kiss her, too. By the time he let her up for air, she was wet and aching.

"Hi, Nina." Zara smiled and hurried over to her as she entered the room. Set and Sab followed close behind, as did Nehi, Menna, Mitry and Weni.

"Hi."

"How are you feeling?" Zara asked.

"Great."

Zara surprised Nina by hugging her. When she stepped back, she scrutinized her intently. "You look so much better. We were all worried about you."

"Apparently, but as you can see, I'm better than normal."

"It's amazing, isn't it? The underlying energy buzzing through your veins."

"Yes, it is. It's going to take a bit to get used to."

"You will. Before you know it, you'll be out and about with your mates and the rest of us."

"I hope so."

Zara winked at her. "You will. Did you get the mark of Ra?"

"What mark?"

Zara pulled the edge of her tank top down, exposing the top of her breast. Nina's mouth dropped open when she saw the eye of Ra on her new friend's skin. It looked just like the tattoo her mates had. Zara lifted her top back up and then did an about-face. Nina moved closer when she saw the image of a falcon tattooed into Zara's left shoulder blade. Her gaze moved to the woman's right shoulder blade and another tattoo-like mark. She studied it closely and saw the eye of Ra was also underneath the falcon and there was also a faint outline in white of what looked like an angel.

"That is so cool," Nina whispered and touched the tattoo mark with her fingertip. A jolt of heat shot through her body and she shuddered before quickly removing her finger. The power surge she'd felt had been so phenomenal it had nearly brought her to her knees.

She glanced over at Pen and Paser to find them staring at her, but when she noticed they were both smiling, her frisson of fear dissipated. Obviously, they were used to feeling such things, and since they weren't concerned about it, she wouldn't be, either.

"Show me yours," Zara said.

"My what?"

"Your mark."

"I don't have—"

"I'll bet you twenty bucks you do."

Nina pulled the hem of her shirt away from her body and her mouth dropped open when she saw she also had the eye of Ra on the top of her left breast.

"Told you."

Nina turned so her back was to Zara. "Do I have…"

Zara tugged the neck of Nina's shirt back toward her, nearly strangling her, but she didn't care about a little discomfort. She wanted to know if she had the mark on her back, too, but she wasn't about to reveal her body to the other men in the room. She didn't think her mates would be too happy if she stood in front of everyone in just her bra.

"Yep, same as mine."

"Why do we have an angel and our mates don't?"

"I don't know. We'll have to ask Ra next time he comes for a visit."

"He visits?" Nina gulped and her belly fluttered with nerves.

"Yeah. Don't worry, though. He's cool."

"If you say so."

"Nothing?" Pen sounded astounded.

"What's going on?" Nina asked as she and Zara walked over to where the men were chatting.

"We didn't find any demonic." Zara frowned.

"That's good, isn't it?"

"Not necessarily," Set answered.

"Why not?"

"There hasn't been a night in our five thousand years as sentinels where we haven't had to fight at least one shadow demon," Mit explained.

"So maybe you're winning," Nina said.

Sab shook his head. "No. More likely, Apep and his minions are planning."

"Why here?" Nina asked.

"What, baby?" Pen slung and arm around her shoulder and pulled her against him.

"Why are you based here, in Utah?"

"For some reason, this area has always been the demonic's playground," Wen replied.

"Yes, but why?"

"That's a good question," Mit smiled at her before gazing at everyone else. His gaze stopped on Set. "And I think it's one we need to find the answer to."

"Maybe you could ask Ra?"

"Ra only ever tells us what we need to know and nothing more. Sometimes his answers just give us more questions," Nehi said.

"So you think that Apep is building an army?" Nina asked, and while she hoped she was wrong, the knot of dread in her gut said otherwise.

"Maybe." Paser scowled.

"We'll be ready for them," Set said.

Nina hoped that he was right, but she couldn't shake the bad feeling in her stomach.

Chapter Twelve

Paser hated leaving Nina back at base each time he and Pen went out with the other sentinels in search of the shadow demons, but he was grateful that Zara had volunteered to keep her company and help to train her how to fight.

It had been a week since Nina had been transformed, and each day she was getting stronger and stronger. Now that he had her, he never wanted her out of his sight, but he couldn't shirk his duties because he was feeling overprotective.

What worried him, though, was that the shadow demons had been quiet. Too quiet. They had only encountered one demon or possessed human a night, and even though it was great to not have to fight as much, he didn't like it.

"There's something coming," Pen murmured as they headed back to the base. "The hair on the back of my neck won't go down and my gut's telling me not to let my guard down."

"Yeah, I feel the same way."

"Let's go see our mate," Pen said before he sprinted away. Paser took off after him. He was eager to hold Nina in his arms again. He needed to make love to her until she screamed with pleasure. There was nothing more arousing than having Nina come around his cock or hearing her cries of pleasure. He smiled and adjusted his hard dick to a more comfortable position.

He would be holding Nina in his arms very soon.

* * * *

Nina couldn't believe how much progress she'd made in her training in seven days. She and Zara had spent each and every night sparring and sword-fighting with each other, and she felt as if she were ready to go out and fight at her mates' sides.

"You're a natural." Zara lowered the sword to her side. "I think you handle that sword better than I do."

"I don't' know about that." Nina placed her sword back in the rack on the wall.

"I do. I haven't been able to break through your defense once and you broke mine twice." Zara sighed and pushed her hair back from her face before glancing at her watch. "The guys should be back soon. I'm going to have a shower before they get back."

"Me too."

"I'll see you in a bit," Zara said before heading out.

Nina glanced about the room and shivered. The gym was bright because of the fluorescent lights overhead, but all of a sudden she felt as if it were full of shadows, darkness. Just as she started to get scared, the lights flickered and then went out.

She edged toward the doorway but stopped when she thought she saw something move in the far corner of the room. When she squinted to try and see what it was, all she could see was black. Fear made her heart pound in her chest and her legs began to tremble. She tried to push the fear back down and convince herself she was only imagining things, but she'd never been afraid of the dark before.

Ice and heat warred in her body and she began to inch her way back to the hallway again, keeping her eyes on the corner. She was no more than five feet from the door when it slammed behind her. The lock engaging was so loud she jumped and nearly fell onto her knees.

A cold breeze brushed over the back of her neck and she whimpered but quickly shuffled away toward where the swords were hanging on the wall. She chanced a glance back over her shoulder toward the now-closed-and-locked door and froze when she saw black, wispy shadows swirling in the air. Now that she'd mated and been transformed, she didn't need a light on to see. It had taken all of five seconds for her eyes to adjust to the lack of light, but right now she wished she couldn't see a thing.

There were at least five shadow demons in the room and she was scared spit-less, her mouth as dry as the most arid desert on the planet. She managed to get to her feet and her fingers were inches away from the sword, but she was too late. The shadows were on her before she could take her next breath, and though she opened her mouth to scream, nothing came out.

Evil, oily blackness enfolded her in its clutches and she couldn't even draw in another deep breath. Her chest was so tight if felt like it was being crushed, and the pain as those five shadows encased her whole body in their hold and tugged at her chest was pure, unadulterated agony.

Pain shot up through her knees when she landed on them on the floor, but she hadn't even felt her knees buckle. She was burning alive from the inside and yet she was also so cold her bones were aching.

She tried to move, but she couldn't break the shadow demon's hold and she was fighting a losing battle. Tears streamed down her face, and while she was terrified she was about to die and wanted to scream, she couldn't. She remembered that Zara was in the building, too, and hoped the other woman wasn't aware the demons were here. She didn't want her new friend to be hurt or end up dying, too.

Pen's and Paser's face shimmered in her consciousness, and as she fell to the floor face-down, she prayed they would be okay and continue to fight and live without her. Then everything went black.

* * * *

"Something's wrong." Pen rubbed at his chest and ran faster. "Nina!"

Paser and Pen overtook the other sentinels and barely stopped to open the door to the base. Pen ignored the burning in his palm as electricity surged through his body. Although it hurt like hell and would have normally brought him to his knees, it was inconsequential to what he was feeling coming from his mate.

"They're inside," Paser shouted before following Pen along the hallway. "Where is she?"

"The gym." Pen stopped at the door, turned the handle and pushed, but the door wouldn't budge. His heart was hammering in his chest, and he was filled with rage, but he was also scared out of his mind. Their mate was in trouble. He needed to get to her, protect her and make sure she was okay.

"Stand back." Pen moved across to the far side of the hall and then ran straight at it. His shoulder slammed into metal, and though it hurt like a son of a bitch, he wasn't giving up.

"Let me try. One after the other." Paser shoved Pen aside and then aimed at the door. Again and again they battered on the metal, but it wouldn't budge.

"Zara!" Set and Sab yelled at the same time, but Pen ignored them. They needed to get the fucking door open.

"What's wrong?" Zara came out into the hallway.

"Thank God," Set said.

"Let me try," En nudged Pen aside and kicked at the door with his foot right next to the door handle.

"Where's Nina?" Sab asked.

"We were in the gym. She was going to have a shower. Oh god, are they here?"

"We think they have Nina, baby," Set said.

"It's not working," En said in a growly voice.

"Can you feel her?" Pen asked Paser, blinking rapidly when the back of his eyes burned.

"Yes, but she's getting fainter," Paser yelled. "What the hell are we supposed to do? How can we save our mate if we can't get to her?"

Zara walked up and stopped in front of them, reached out and touched their arms. "I know you're worried and scared, but you need to calm down. You can't go in there half-cocked. You'll end up getting yourselves killed, and what good will that do your mate?"

"We need to get to her," Pen yelled and took a deep breath when he realized he was being unreasonable. "I'm sorry."

"Don't apologize. Calm down and then use your brains."

"Move out of the way," Men said as he shoved through and moved up close to the door.

"What..." Pen didn't finish his question because he already had his answer. Men was prying the pins from the hinges.

He held his breath until his lungs began to burn and pulled in a gasp of air. The moment the pins were removed, Pen expected the door to move, but it remained fast. Men rose to his feet and pushed against the metal, and again it didn't move. The fucking door should have opened as soon as the last pin had been extracted.

"Pen," Paser whispered as he slid down the wall to his ass. "I can't feel her anymore."

Pen staggered and went to his knees. The tears he'd been holding at bay welled and flowed down his cheeks. "Nina!" he roared with grief and rage. The emotions were so overwhelming he could barely keep himself together. He felt like his heart, soul and body were being ripped in half. He was only vaguely aware of Zara's quiet sobs and sniffles.

* * * *

Paser didn't care that his face was wet with his tears, the pain in his chest was agony, but he couldn't give up, couldn't believe that Nina was dead. Just because he couldn't feel her through the connection, that didn't mean she had died. It couldn't, because there was no way he would be able to survive without her. He sat on the floor, drew in a couple of deep breaths and pictured his mate's beautiful face, the love and warmth he felt whenever they were together and the love he held in his heart for her.

At first, her face was a little blurry, but as he concentrated on the emotions, the love he had for her, her face became clearer. He reached out, grabbed his friend's hand and hoped Pen could feel and see what he was. If they could reconnect with Nina's heart and soul, maybe they could save her and get her back.

* * * *

Even though her eyes were open, she could see nothing but thick blackness. Her teeth were chattering together and she was so cold her nose was running. If she could have seen, she would swear that she would able to see her breath puffing out each time she exhaled.

Nina didn't think she was in the gym anymore, but she wasn't certain. However, she was aware of the cold, hard floor beneath her body, and she could hear a steady drip, drip, drip. Was she in a cave? Maybe a dungeon or a jail?

Other than breathing, her teeth clicking together involuntarily, and blinking, she couldn't move. Her chest felt like she had an elephant sitting on it and if she didn't know any better, she would swear she had broken limbs. All she could remember was those terrifying shadows wrapping around her and then total oblivion.

Nina wanted to go home. She wished she was in bed between Pen and Paser, safe and sound, but she couldn't wish away her nightmarish reality no matter how much she wished to. She tried to ignore the scrapes, shuffles moans and screams as best as she could, but no matter how hard she tried to push those sounds to the back of her mind, they kept seeping through.

The air near her head shifted and she blinked when she saw two large, shiny black boots stop right in front of her eyes. A scream trapped in her throat when a cruel hand grabbed a handful of hair on the top of her head, and then she was lifted from the cold, hard ground.

Her breath was rasping in and out of her mouth as adrenaline and fear surged through her veins, but she still couldn't move, and because of that, she couldn't flee or fight. The moment her eyes connected with those evil, soulless ones, her body began to quake even more. Her bladder was full and for a minute she wondered if she would piss her pants.

A hysterical bubble of laughter erupted from her mouth, and while she tried to quell, it she couldn't stop it. All the time she was laughing, she was cursing her insanity.

Way to piss off the demon god, Nina. You have a real death wish.

"Silence," Apep roared so loudly her eardrums vibrated with pain, and when she felt trickles of fluid leak out of her ears, she wondered if they had busted. "What do you find so amusing? Don't you realize the peril you're in?"

"Duh," Nina said and then gasped. She didn't know when she'd gotten her voice back, but she was glad she had. If that was the only way she could fight then so be it. "You're a dickhead."

Apep chuckled and then full-out laughed. She had no idea what he found so funny but she ended up laughing, too. Not because she found her situation amusing, but because she knew if she didn't laugh, she would be screaming and crying with fear. This guy and his minions had already seen enough of her terror and didn't need to see anymore.

"Ra is going to kick your ass."

His laughter grew louder and he dropped her to the ground before doubling over as his mirth continued. When he finally stopped, he grabbed her arms and hauled her to her feet. He must have been controlling her body because she was able to remain standing.

"You reek of those sentinels. Did they fuck you? I'll bet a few of my minions would love to get between your spread thighs."

"You're sick."

"You dare to say such things when you're in such a precarious position? I could snap your neck with the snap of my fingers."

"So what?" Nina said. "You do your worst. I don't care, but the sentinels and Ra won't give up until you and your followers are wiped from the earth and hell. Love is what makes the world go around, not power, greed or violence. I feel sorry for you, Apep. You are so evil you wouldn't know love if it bit you in the ass."

"Shut up!"

"No!" Nina shouted back. "You can torture me and kill me, but you will never win the battle you're waging. Those men fighting your demons love each other and the sun god, Ra. They know what is right, what's good and most importantly of all, they know what love is. You will never know what it's like to have someone care for you, the gentle touch of a hand, the love of a brother to stand at your side. You know nothing but violence and evil, and because of that, you won't win. I love my men with my whole heart and they love me right back. I would die for them and they would die for me. Can you say that about any of these poor, tortured souls? Of course you can't. You don't know what love is. You're pathetic, Apep."

Nina was breathless by the time she'd finished her tirade, and though she cringed over goading the leader of the underworld into killing her, she wouldn't have changed anything that she'd said. She knew without a shadow of a doubt that her guys would take a sword for her just as she would for them.

She looked down when she felt warm moisture trickling over her skin and saw that her clothes had slashes in them and her skin was also cut and weeping blood. She didn't remember getting cut and wondered if the shadow demons had done that when they'd wrapped around her.

When she heard Apep step forward, a strange calmness washed over her. She was no longer afraid. Not of him and not of dying. What worried her was how her mates would survive if she died, but she knew the other sentinels and Zara would do everything they could to help them through their grief. She didn't want to die. She'd only just met her mates and wanted to spend the rest of her long life by their sides, loving with them, fighting with them and caring for them.

Once more, their handsome faces filled her mind. The more she thought of them, her love for them and their love for her, the warmer she felt. They were so handsome and good and just. No wonder Ra had chosen them and their friends to fight against the demon shadows and their leader. Their hearts and souls were attuned to helping others and keeping them safe.

Nina gasped when Apep's huge hand wrapped around her throat and squeezed. She didn't fight him because she knew it was useless to fight someone so much stronger than she was. When he squeezed harder, she relaxed her muscles and poured all the love in her heart up and out toward her mates.

Apep roared in pain, which had Nina snapping her eyes open. The dark, dank chamber was illuminated to every corner and the light was so bright it nearly hurt her eyes. She moved her eyeballs from side to side, trying to see where the light was coming from, and would have gasped if she'd been able to. It was coming from her.

From the look on Apep's face, he was in agony and the grip he had around her neck loosened slightly, giving her a chance to gulp in air. The stench of burning flesh assailed her nostrils, and she wanted to gag but didn't. When she saw smoke wafting up in front of her face, she realized that it was Apep's flesh that was burning.

Nina tried to move her arms. The demon god was still controlling her somehow, but it didn't matter because as she continued to pour her emotions out toward her mates, she felt them in her heart and they sent her all the love in their hearts. The longer they fed each other, the stronger she felt and she was finally able to move. Whatever spell or curse Apep had had on her was broken and she was free.

She didn't even think about what she was doing, but the moment her hands wrapped around Apep's thick wrist, she knew she had done the right thing. He screamed as if he was in agony and tried to pull away. Nina gripped him harder and coughed when smoke entered her mouth, nose and lungs, but she hung on.

A cry left her mouth when a fist slammed into the side of her face, and for a moment, all she could see were dark pinpricks and the light faded, but she clung to Apep with all her might. Her skin began to itch just below her shoulder blades, and even though she wanted to back up to the rock wall and scratch the interminable painful itching, she tried to ignore it.

She was more aware of her mates than she had ever been and felt like they were standing right next to her, offering her their strength and their love. The darkness in her eyes diminished and when she looked up into Apep's eyes, she saw fear. Fear that she was going to kill him. Fear that he and his minions wouldn't win this fight of good versus evil. Fear of her.

Apep managed to get away from her hold, and he turned to flee.

The bright white light began to change color into a deep golden hue. Nina had no idea what was happening but wasn't about to hang around to find out. Apep had just reached a hole in the rock wall and as he stepped through it, he seemed to vanish into thin air. Nina decided it was time to try and get the heck out of here, wherever here was, and she raced toward the entrance.

She didn't make it. Just as she was about to step through the cavity, the golden light got so bright she had to close her eyes, but she had no intention of stopping her flight. She put her hands out in front of her so she didn't go slamming into the rock wall but didn't slow her step.

A loud oomph left her lungs when she slammed up against something big, warm and hard. She tried to stop her forward momentum but she was going too fast. Her outstretched arms bent at the elbows and she ended up with her forearms resting on whatever she'd come into contact with. Her eyes flew open, ready to do battle with Apep's shadow demons or Apep himself again. She wasn't going to give up.

She was determined to get out of here and back with her mates where she belonged.

Chapter Thirteen

"Why can't we get in?" Pen shouted, and then grunted as he ran at the door again. Pain radiated into his shoulder and down his arm. He stepped back, not willing to give up until he had Nina in his arms, until he knew she was safe.

"I don't know," Paser replied just as loudly. He ran his fingers through his hair and began to pace agitatedly.

"Can't you feel it?" Zara said as she, Set and Sab moved closer to the closed gym door.

"The evil?" En asked with a frown before nodding.

"Yes, but it's more than I've ever felt before." Zara moved closer to the door and placed her palm on it. She gasped and snatched her hand back. When she turned around to face them, the fear on her face and emanating from her body was palpable. "The evil is so thick I'm almost choking on it."

"I can only feel what we normally do," Set said before gently moving Zara aside and then he, too, placed his palm on the door. He shook his head with confusion. "It doesn't feel any different than when we're facing the shadow demons."

Pen stepped toward Zara and would have grabbed hold of her hand if Sab hadn't knocked his away. The other man glared at him so hard he probably should have shriveled up and died, but he didn't care. All that mattered was saving his mate. He ignored Sab's glare and the low growl he let loose and concentrated on Zara.

"What do you feel?"

"The evil is thick and oily like it normally is, but there's also heat and ice. I can't decide if I want to shiver or fan myself. When I touched the door, it was as if a physical pain manifested in my chest and the evil oiliness was seeping into my body, heart and soul. It was really hard to fill my lungs with air."

"Fuck!" Paser snarled. "Do you think Apep is in there?"

"I don't know," Zara whispered fearfully, "but this is more than we've ever dealt with before."

"Maybe we could punch through the wall," Mitry suggested.

"Let's do it," Pen agreed. "We can't do nothing. We have to get to Nina."

Pen shoved Set and Sab out of the way and, without any thought, punched through the plaster wall. He didn't even flinch when he felt the skin on his knuckles split and start bleeding. Nothing mattered but Nina.

Paser moved to his side and joined him. His fist punched after his. It took them three punches between the both of them to get through to the other side, but the moment Pen's hand went through the second piece of Gyprock, he had to bite back a howl of pain. He'd come up against what felt like a brick wall, and since he wasn't human and stronger than any living creature alive, it shouldn't have stopped him from going through the barrier.

Paser cursed as his punch followed Pen's. "What the fuck is going on?"

"I think Apep is doing this." Zara's voice cracked with fear.

Pen had never been so scared in his life. He'd thought Nina being sick had been fear-inducing, but that was nothing compared to the terror he was feeling right now. If Apep had their mate…He couldn't complete that thought. He couldn't even contemplate losing Nina. It would utterly destroy him if he did. It would destroy both him and Paser.

"Ra!" Pen shouted. It was time the sun god helped them out. There was no way Pen, Paser or any of the others could get into the underworld. They had no idea how to and had never even tried to, but if he needed to visit the bowels of hell to save his mate, he would do so without a qualm.

"Ra!" Paser yelled and turned in a circle as if expecting the sun god to appear at their summons.

Pen roared with fury when their summons went unanswered. Panic warred with rage in his heart. He, Paser and the others had fought for Ra for thousands of years, and now that they needed him like they'd never needed him before, he had the audacity to ignore them. Something inside of him broke in that instant. He wondered if the trust and loyalty he'd had for Ra over the millennia had been misdirected. Pen gripped his hair and tugged. He felt like he'd been betrayed and the only thing keeping him sane was pain, pain and anger that seemed to escalate each time his heart beat, each time he took a breath.

"Why won't he come?" Zara asked, the last word ending on a sob.

Set and Sab pulled their mate between them as she cried.

Pen felt like an asshole because he knew Zara was hurting, worried for her friend, but that was nothing to what he was feeling. She had her mates with her and they had her. He couldn't listen or watch the loving interaction without doing or saying something he may end up regretting.

He turned away and strode toward Ra's temple. His heart was thumping hard against his chest and he was breathing heavy. He didn't pant even when he was fighting the shadow demons.

Pen knew Paser was following, but he couldn't acknowledge his friend right now. They were closer than ever before thanks to Nina, but she wasn't here and he was having a hard enough time dealing with his own pain, fear and grief, and didn't need the connection he had with Paser and have to deal with his friend's pain, too.

The moment he entered Ra's temple, he yelled his name again. He stood beneath the lightening sky and called to his deity until he was hoarse. Paser's voice joined his, but Ra remained silent. Pen sank to his knees, aware of Paser doing the same, and then he bowed his head and prayed. He prayed like he'd never prayed in his life.

Just when he was about to give up hope, he felt a tingling warmth in the region of his heart. He looked inward and when he saw the spark of pure white light, he knew that Nina was still alive.

He brought her face to his mind and the love he had for her filled his heart.

"I can feel her," Paser whispered hesitantly, as if scared his voice would break the slight connection they could feel with their mate.

"So can I." Pen reached over, clasped Paser's shoulder and squeezed. The moment his hand touched his friend, the bond with their mate grew stronger.

When he heard a rustle, he looked toward the door and found the other sentinels and Zara standing against the wall.

One by one, the other sentinels stepped forward to surround him and Paser. They placed their hands on their shoulders, arms anywhere they could reach. Zara ducked under Set's arm and leaned back against him and Sab before she reached out and placed her hands on the top of Pen's and Paser's heads.

Pen jolted as love and warmth surged through his body and from the way Paser shuddered, he felt it, too.

"The bonds getting stronger," Pen said in a hoarse voice. He glanced up at Set, Sab and Zara, and smiled, not giving a shit when he felt tears roll down his cheeks. The moment the others touched him and Paser, the link to Nina snapped back into place.

He bit back a sob when he felt her love for them seeping through his pores into his skin and flowing into his heart.

"She's drawing on our strength, on our bond and our love," Paser said, awe in his voice.

"Don't pull away," Pen ordered the others. He closed his eyes and centered his entire being on Nina.

He felt her anger and fear, but then the fear just seemed to evaporate. The anger grew, as did the love and purity of her soul until it was streaming through his body. The power flowed and rose until he wanted to shout with joy, but he didn't want anything to break the renewed connection he and Paser had with their mate.

Pen grit his teeth when he felt pain, but he knew it wasn't his. It was Nina's. He wanted to howl with fury, but he didn't. He contained his rage and centered his being on the love between the three of them and the love he had for his comrades. His whole body seemed to fill with power, his muscles growing hard as blood pumped through his veins. There was a massive surge and he swore he heard a scream of agony and fear, but it wasn't Nina's, nor had it come from anyone in the room with him and Paser.

Nina was winning the battle she was waging and he knew he would have her back in his arms, between him and Paser, very soon. It was the most humbling experience in his long existence. He'd thought he knew what love and caring was, but he hadn't, not really, not until Nina had come into his life, and when he had her back in his arms, he was going to make sure she knew how much he loved and cherished her.

He knew the moment she won her battle and turned to flee, but when he felt her awe, he wondered what was going on. The moment he opened his eyes and met Paser's gaze, they smiled at each other, but then Pen's smile faded. If Apep and the shadow demons had taken her into the underworld, he wasn't sure how they would get her back, but as that thought crossed his mind, his diminishing belief in Ra surged to the fore again.

Ra wouldn't have sent Nina to them only to be taken away after only just mating her. He closed his eyes in contrition and prayed to Ra, praying that the god would forgive him his moments of doubt.

"Do you think it was a test?" Paser asked.

Pen's eyes snapped open again, and even though his answer had been on the tip of his tongue, it never found voice. The room was awash in the brightest glow he'd ever seen. His heart flipped and he gasped air into his lungs.

"What's happening?" Zara asked in a whisper, but no one answered her.

A crack of thunder boomed, vibrating the entire compound. A streak of lightening hit the top of the glass pyramid through the thin layer of water covering it and then shot down straight down, hitting him and Paser. His mouth opened on a scream, but more from shock than pain, although no sound emerged from his lips. Every single one of them was bathed in a mixture of white and gold light.

He didn't notice when the others had stopped touching him and Paser until they began to back away from them. Pen wanted to get to his feet, but he was too awed to move. Warmth encased his body in a loving embrace and he blinked to keep more tears from spilling down his face. He was sure he'd only had his eyes closed for a brief moment, but when he opened them, he was looking at his mate and Ra.

Ra had Nina cradled in his arms as if she were a precious babe. He took a step toward him and Paser, and then he knelt. He kissed Nina's forehead and, with the utmost care, handed her over to them. Pen and Paser moved so their bodies touched, side to side, and cradled Nina between them.

Her clothes had slashes in them and were covered in blood, but she was breathing and he couldn't feel any pain coming from her. She was sleeping deeply and calmly as if she hadn't just fought against shadow demons and the evil god. She looked so peaceful and content, and there was a slight smile on her lips.

"Safe," she sighed and snuggled deeper into him and Paser.

"Your mate is strong, pure and worthy, as are her mates," Ra said in a strong voice. "She fought hard and well and conquered the leader of the underworld."

Pen swallowed around the lump in his throat and nodded. He had no idea what his mate had been through, but after he and Paser made sure she wasn't hurt and she was rested, he intended to find out.

"Her heart is full of her mates and their friends." Ra rose to his feet and looked at the other sentinels and Zara. "Your women are strong and more sensitive to the demonic than you are. Listen to them and learn from them. Each of you have or will be tested.

"The final confrontation is near and it's up to you all whether the battle will be won." Ra once more met everyone's gazes, then he bent over and stroked a finger down Nina's cheek before he straightened again. As he backed away, his body became almost transparent and then he faded completely.

"That was…" Zara's voice carried to him and Paser.

"Is she all right?" Mitry asked as he strode over to them.

"She seems to be."

"Is she unconscious?" En asked as he came to stand beside Mit.

"She's sleeping."

"What the hell happened to her?" Zara asked as she hurried over and then knelt. She brushed Nina's hair back from her forehead. "She's covered in blood but I don't see any wounds."

"I think Ra might have healed her," Set said as he and Sab came up on either side of Zara.

"What I want to know is how the hell the demonic were able to get in here," Weni snarled.

"You're right." Menna frowned down at Nina. "The protection Ra put in place shouldn't have been able to be breached."

Pen was worried about that, too, but he was more concerned for Nina. He felt as if they had failed her. If they hadn't left her alone while he and the others had been out fighting, she wouldn't have been hurt. "We failed her."

"We did."

"What the fuck are you talking about?" Sab asked.

"We left her and Zara alone, and because we did, the shadow demons and the leader of the underworld were able to get her."

"You can't blame yourselves for what happened," Zara met Pen's and then Paser's gazes. "Those assholes seem to be able to move about to wherever they want. What I want to know is why I didn't feel them here."

"I think Apep may have been blocking," Set said. "That's why we couldn't get into the gym."

"But why Nina?" Zara asked.

"What do you mean, mate?" Sab pulled Zara against his side and slung an arm over her shoulders.

"Why did the demonic only go after Nina? I was here alone, too."

"I think I can answer that." Paser shifted Nina's head onto his thigh. "Although we mated Nina and she knows we love her, she doubted herself."

"How?" Mit asked. "She's gorgeous."

"Yes, she is." Pen sighed. "She doubted that she was good enough for us. We got a glimpse of that before we mated and after it was stronger."

"But she knows you love her and she loves you," Nehi stated unequivocally. "You would have all felt that through the bond."

"We did," Pen replied. "We do, but she doesn't or didn't see herself as anyone special. I think the doubts plaguing her mind, heart and soul made her easy prey."

"You could be right." Zara tapped her chin with her fingernail. "She's a fierce warrior with a natural ability, and I told her she was ready to fight by your sides and was a good with the scimitar, but she didn't believe me."

"So even though she had to battle with the shadow demons and Apep, she had to battle with herself more?" Weni asked.

"Yes," Pen answered.

"Shit! That would have been hard," Menna stated.

"We all went through the same thing," Set said. "We all doubted our own abilities when Ra first turned us into demigods."

"Yeah." Nehi sighed as he ran his fingers through his hair. "It was so long ago, I'd forgotten about that."

"Do you think the shadow demons and Apep were able to get in because Ra let them?" Zara asked.

Pen's first instinct was to deny that, but he wasn't so sure. Over the last five thousand or so years, not once had their underground base been infiltrated by the shadow demons or their leader. Ra had told them thousands of years ago that they would be safe in their home and that no demonic or other demigod would be able to get inside without his say-so. So that meant that Ra had let whatever happened to Nina happen.

Anger surged through him, but he swallowed it back down. The sun god wouldn't do anything without a reason. He hated that Nina would have been scared out of her mind and that she'd obviously been hurt, but now that he could think about things logically since his terror for his mate was gone, he couldn't remain pissed.

"I do." Pen finally remembered to answer Zara's question.

Nina sighed and the smile on her face grew before her eyes blinked open. She reached up and cupped Paser's cheek before meeting his gaze.

"Are you all right, baby?" He clasped the hand she reached out to him, threaded his fingers through hers and brought it up to his mouth. He kissed the back of it and then rubbed his cheek over her soft skin.

"I'm fine."

"We were so worried about you," Paser said in a husky voice.

"I was worried about me, too, there for a while."

"Can you tell us what happened, baby?"

"I will but first I want to go and take a shower. I feel like I was dunked in evil and I want to wash the stench from my body. And then I want food. I'm starving."

"We'll see to the food," Zara said as she took hold of her men's hands and tugged them toward the door. "Mit and Wen can set the table. En and Men can make the coffee."

"Give us an hour," Pen called out as he and Paser helped Nina to sit up.

"I don't need that long to wash up." Nina shifted to her knees and then hooked her arms around Pen's and Paser's necks.

"You might not, but we do." Paser hugged Nina around the waist with an arm.

Nina drew back, and after looking into Paser's heated gaze and then meeting his, she giggled.

The sound was so soft and feminine, but also carefree. He'd never heard her so lighthearted before and he knew then that everything was going to be all right.

She released her hold on them, got to her feet and started walking toward the door. "Last one in has to kiss my as...feet."

Pen made a low, growly noise and shoved to his feet. He wanted to be last so he could kiss every sweet inch of her delectable body. Her feet would only be the beginning. Maybe he should have told them to hold breakfast for two hours instead of one.

Paser stood at the same time he did, but neither of them took a step toward the door.

"The longer we stand here, the less time we have to love our woman." Paser winked, shoved Pen back and took off in a blur of speed.

Pen chuckled as he followed. By the time he got to their apartment, he was laughing outright. He was relieved to have Nina back and the connection between them was stronger than ever. There was no doubt left in his mate's heart, none at all.

There was love, however, so much of it that flowed between the three of them, he wondered how his body could contain such joy.

He had so much to look forward to.

Chapter Fourteen

Nina pushed her empty plate back with a sigh. She was satiated in more ways than one. She wrapped her hands around her coffee and looked up when she realized everyone was quiet.

"What?"

"Do you feel okay?" Paser asked with a frown. He placed his hand on her forehead as if checking to see if she had a temperature.

"I'm fine. Stop fussing."

"You're our mate, it's our job to fuss," Pen said in a firm voice.

"I know, and thank you for caring about me."

"We more than care for you, sweetheart." Paser removed his hand and kissed her temple.

Nina smiled, kissed Paser's then Pen's cheek, took a deep breath and then started talking. She didn't stop until she'd told them about Apep's disappearance and her running.

"Did you know where you were?" Zara asked.

"Other than underground? No."

"So how did you get out?" Set picked Zara up from her seat and, as he scooted his chair back, plonked her on his lap and wrapped his arms around her waist.

"I didn't." Nina took a sip of her coffee and licked the residual moisture from her lips before she continued. "The light was so bright I couldn't see. There was a pure white light emanating from me, and just before Apep escaped, a bright golden glow joined mine. I had to close my eyes because it blinded me, but I didn't stop running. I just held my hands out in front of me and kept right on going. When I bumped into something big and solid I opened my eyes and there was

Ra. He was so big and intimidating, but for some reason I was neither scared nor intimidated."

"What happened next?" Mit leaned forward in his chair, staring at her avidly.

"I'm not really certain." Nina cleared her throat and tried not to shudder, but when Paser lifted her to his lap, she knew she'd failed to hide her reaction. "Shadow demons came out of nowhere and they were everywhere. There were so many of them I couldn't count, and as I went to back away, they swarmed around Ra and me. Ra didn't seem to be concerned at all. He smiled, held his hand out to me and waited. I grabbed hold of his hand and I think I must have passed out for a bit or something, because when I opened my eyes again, the demonic were gone.

"I was about to ask Ra what had happened but a loud, angry scream echoed through the caves, and then he swept me up in his arms. The next thing I knew, I was waking up draped over Pen and Paser."

"Do you think Ra took care of the shadow demons?" Zara asked.

Nina shrugged because she couldn't answer that question with any certainty. "I don't know, and while I suspect he did, I don't really care. All that matters is I'm back where I belong."

"I'll agree with that." En smiled and winked at her.

Nina tried to smother her yawn, but she leaned her cheek on Paser's shoulder and sighed when his arms surrounded her. She was encompassed in his heat and his love.

"Are you all going hunting tonight?" Nina asked.

"No," Pen answered. "You need to rest."

"I'm fine."

"You may be, but it's going to take us a long time to recover after what happened. We're never going to leave you alone again." Paser ran his fingers through her hair.

"Does that mean you're going to take me with you from now on?"

"You're more than ready." Pen nodded.

"But not tonight?" Nina questioned.

"No, not tonight." Paser turned her until she was sitting in his lap side-on and then hooked her knees over his arm, braced her back against his other arm, and stood.

"We're going to spend the day with our mate. You all are free to do whatever you want, but no one will be going out to hunt the demonic. We all deserve some time to unwind." Pen took the lead and Paser followed, taking her with him.

Paser lowered her to the bed, but when he went to draw away, Nina clung to him. She loved him and Pen so much, and no matter how many times they made love to her, it was never enough.

"What's wrong, sweetheart?" Paser nibbled on her neck.

"Nothing. I love it when you touch me, make love to me. I need you."

"Are you sure you aren't too tired?" Pen asked as he sat on the edge of the bed.

Paser drew back but she was glad when he sat beside her, too.

"I'll never be too tired to make love with my mates. I love you both so much."

Paser rose, turned to face her and tugged the hem of his shirt up and over his head. She glanced over at Pen when he stood and saw that he was quickly removing his clothes, too. Nina whipped her shirt off, unhooked her bra and then flung both at Pen. He chuckled at her antics, but the sound was deep and husky with his desire, and from his heated gaze, he needed her just as much as she needed him and Paser.

Her body didn't seem to care that they had made love only a couple hours ago and she knew it was because of the deep love they held for each other. The hunger would always be there simmering beneath the surface, ready to flare up at a look or a touch.

She pushed her sweat pants down over her hips, taking her panties with them, and was grateful she only had a pair of socks on her feet and no shoes to deal with. She flung her pants and panties at a now-naked Paser and he growled playfully as he snatched them out of the air. The sweats were dropped to the floor, but he brought her panties up to his nose and inhaled deeply.

"I love the sweet smell of your cunt, sweetheart. I am going to lick and suck on that wet little pussy until you scream my name."

"Oh," Nina moaned, the socks still on her feet, completely forgotten.

Pen crawled up onto the bed bedside her and as she turned to him, he reached for her. Their mouths meshed and clung as the passion began to build. His mouth opened over hers and his tongue delved deep before gliding along and twirling around hers. She threaded her fingers into his hair and held on tight as she lost herself in his heat, touch, taste and love.

She mewled when Paser got on the mattress between her splayed thighs and shivered when he caressed up the inside of her legs, stopping just short of her wet pussy, before making the journey back down. He removed her socks and then maneuvered until he was comfortable.

Nina smoothed a hand down over Pen's shoulder, chest and pectoral and ripped abs, seeing the defined delineation of his muscles in her mind as she touched his body. When her hand brushed over the moist tip of his hard cock, she caressed his erection lightly with the tips of her fingers before wrapping them around the base. She pumped her hand up and down, delighting in the groans and moans he breathed into her mouth.

Paser pressed against the inside of her upper thighs and then he lowered his head. Her body tautened with excited anticipation, but it seemed that her mate was in no hurry. He blew over her engorged clit, causing her cunt to clench and goose bumps to race over her skin.

Pen released her lips, licking and nibbling down her neck and the upper slope of first one breast and then the other. She arched her hips and chest one after the other, begging her mates to touch her. Pen chuckled right before he laved one aching nub with the tip of his tongue before moving over to the other to tease.

Paser rimmed her pussy with his finger before gliding up and down each side of her folds until she thought she would go mad with desire.

A loud moan left her parted lips when they both struck at the same time. Pen sucked her nipple into his mouth, drawing on the peak with short, sharp pulls which turned her into a writhing mass of need. Paser pressed a finger deep into her cunt as he flicked his tongue over her clit before he added another and began to pump them in and out of her cunt.

Nina moaned and gasped. She pumped Pen's cock faster, hoping to take one of her mates with her, but he pried her fingers from his hard dick and pressed her hand up beside her head.

"Why?" she gasped her question.

"I want to be inside of you when I come, baby."

"Oh! Yes!" Nina cried as she tipped over the edge into orgasm.

Paser continued to slide his fingers in and out of her pussy, driving her orgasm higher as he flicked and lapped at her clit. When she started to come back down, he removed his finger from her pussy and then shoved his tongue in deep, sucking up all of her juices.

"Fucking delicious," Paser growled as he sat up. "Are you ready for us, sweetheart."

"Yes. Now!" Nina reached out toward him as he aligned his dick with her pussy. Pen shifted away from her, giving her and Paser room, but she didn't want him going anywhere. She wanted both her mates making love to her at the same time. "Don't go."

"I'm not going anywhere, baby. Just giving Paser room to move."

"Oh," Nina groaned as Paser began to enter her cunt with his cock.

He lowered his body to hers, bracing his weight on his elbows, and then he slanted his mouth over hers as he surged deep into her pussy.

The kiss they shared was hot, wet, wild and passionate, but she needed more. She needed him to move. She needed Pen to fill her ass.

Her nails dug into his shoulders as fiery lust raced through her body, causing her to shake.

"Hold on to me, sweetheart," Paser ordered breathlessly, and when she'd done as he'd asked, he rolled them both over.

"So good," she whimpered. In this position, with her on top of Paser, his cock was inside so deep she was sure he'd breached her womb, but it still wasn't enough.

Pen's hand caressed up and down her back and then over her ass cheeks. She moaned and wiggled in invitation. He chuckled and then slapped her ass, one cheek and then the other. Nina's cunt clenched and dripped cream.

"Do that again," Paser ordered. "She just covered my cock with her cream."

Pen slapped both cheeks alternately and then he gripped her hips as he moved up closer to her. "I love you, baby."

"I love you, too."

The tip of Pen's lubed cock pressed against her ass and she moaned as the head breached her.

"So fucking good. So hot and tight," Pen rasped.

Nina took a deep breath and as Pen stroked in she pushed back with her muscles. They both moaned when his pubis connected with her ass. Her breath came in short, heavy pants and she tried to wriggle her hips to get her men to move.

Pen eased back from her ass in a long, gentle retreat, and as he drove back in, Paser withdrew from her pussy. With each stroke in and out of her anus and cunt, they increased the pace of their thrusts until their bodies were slapping against hers.

The heat in her veins got hotter. The friction of their cocks gliding in and out of her holes grew warmer and the tension in her body grew tauter.

Nina moaned and gasped when Paser cupped her breasts before pinching and plucking her hard nipples. Pen gripped her hip with one hand while he skimmed the other down over her belly to the top of her slit. His finger delved into her folds and the top of her cunt to press over her swollen clit.

The pressure on her clitoris was enough to send her racing up the slope to the precipice where she hovered on the threshold for a couple of seconds.

Paser slid his cock from her pussy to the tip, Pen did the same with his cock till the crown was resting just inside of her anus, and as she drew in a ragged breath, they both shoved into her at the same time.

Nina screamed as she toppled over the edge. Her body shook and shuddered. Her internal walls clenched and released before clamping down again. Cream dripped from her cunt and spilled from her body as her mates pounded their cocks in and out of her ass and pussy. The more she climaxed, the faster they pumped their hips until they fucked her through one climax and up in to another.

Pen drove into her ass with a roar, holding his cock deep as he orgasmed. His cock twitched and jerked as he spumed load after load into her back entrance. Paser growled low in his throat as he powered up into her pussy, once, twice, three times, and then held still with a shout as his warm seed shot out of his pulsing dick and deep into her cunt and womb.

Nina collapsed onto Paser's, chest gasping for breath, her body still quaking and quivering with aftershocks.

Pen drew his softening cock from her ass and headed toward the bathroom. She heard water running and when Paser rolled them both to their sides, his cock slipped from her pussy. Pen returned with a warm, damp cloth and, after cleaning her up, got into bed beside her.

"Love you, baby."

"Love you," she sighed.

"Love you, sweetheart." Paser kissed her shoulder as he pulled her closer against him, and she kissed his shoulder.

"Love you, too."

Nina drifted on a cloud of satiated desire and love as her mates cuddled her between them.

She didn't know what they would have to deal with against the shadow demons and Apep, but one thing she was certain about was that she wouldn't want to change a thing. They wouldn't give up and she had a feeling in the end they would be victorious.

She loved her two mates and they loved her, and that was all that mattered in the scheme of things. Friends, family and love were the most important facets in life.

Everything else was inconsequential.

Pen and Paser were the light of her life, the very air she breathed. She loved them so much and couldn't wait to begin the rest of her life with her men beside her.

THE END

WWW.BECCAVAN-EROTICROMANCE.COM

ABOUT THE AUTHOR

My name is Becca Van. I live in Australia with my wonderful hubby of many years, as well as my two children.

I read my first romance, which I found in the school library, at the age of thirteen and haven't stopped reading them since. It is so wonderful to know that love is still alive and strong when there seems to be so much conflict in the world.

I dreamed of writing my own book one day but, unfortunately, didn't follow my dream for many years. But once I started, I knew writing was what I wanted to continue doing.

I love to escape from the world and curl up with a good romance to see how the characters unfold and conflict is dealt with. I have read many books and love all facets of the romance genre, from historical to erotic romance. I am a sucker for a happy ending.

For all titles by Becca Van, please visit
www.bookstrand.com/becca-van

Siren Publishing, Inc.
www.SirenPublishing.com

Lightning Source UK Ltd.
Milton Keynes UK
UKOW06f2356170816

280960UK00021B/676/P